On the
Victory
Trail

Other Books in the Keystone Stables Series

On the Victory Trail

BOOK 2

KEYSTONE
Stables

Formerly titled *A True Test for Skye*

..... *Marsha Hubler* .....

ZONDERkidz

ZONDERVAN.com/
AUTHORTRACKER
follow your favorite authors

Zonderkidz

On the Victory Trail
Formerly titled *A True Test for Skye*
Copyright © 2004, 2009 by Marsha Hubler

Requests for information should be addressed to:
Zonderkidz, *Grand Rapids, MI 49530*

Library of Congress Cataloging-in-Publication Data

Hubler, Marsha, 1947-
  [True test for Skye]
  On the victory trail / by Marsha Hubler.
    p. cm. — (Keystone Stables ; bk. 2)
  Summary: The love of her foster parents, her friend Morgan, and her own
devotion to the horses and dogs at Keystone Stables help Skye become a
Christian and to, in turn, find a way to help her troubled friend Sooze.
  ISBN 978-0-310-71793-5 (softcover)
  [1. Foster home care—Fiction. 2. Horses—Fiction. 3. Christian life—Fiction.
4. Friendship—Fiction. 5. Death—Fiction.] I. Title. II. Series.
  PZ7.H86325On 2010
  [Fic]—dc22   2008053937

All Scripture quotations, unless otherwise indicated, are taken from the
Holy Bible, New International Version®. NIV®. Copyright © 1973, 1978, 1984
by International Bible Society. Used by permission of Zondervan. All rights
reserved.

Any Internet addresses (websites, blogs, etc.) and telephone numbers printed
in this book are offered as a resource. They are not intended in any way to be
or imply an endorsement by Zondervan, nor does Zondervan vouch for the
content of these sites and numbers for the life of this book.

Interior illustrator: Lyn Boyer
Interior design and composition: Carlos Estrada and Sherri L. Hoffman

Printed in the United States of America

09 10 11 12 13 • 5 4 3 2

*In memory of Beth Barnhart
who lost her battle with a brain tumor but
won the victory on October 30, 1999.*

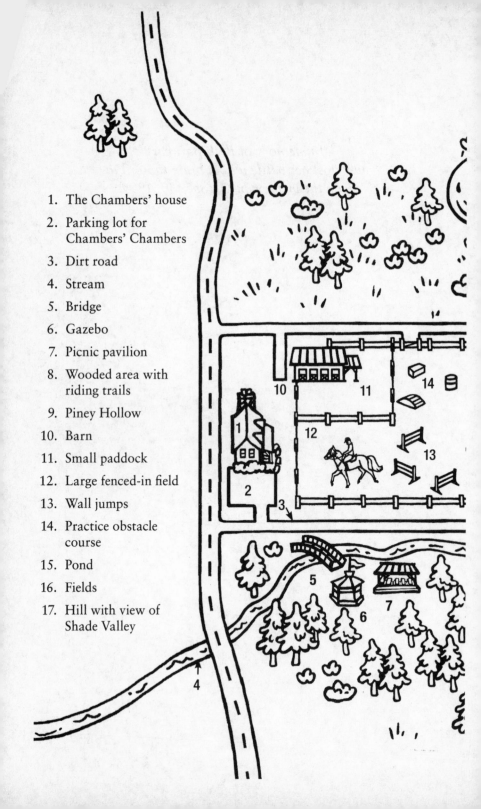

1. The Chambers' house

2. Parking lot for Chambers' Chambers

3. Dirt road

4. Stream

5. Bridge

6. Gazebo

7. Picnic pavilion

8. Wooded area with riding trails

9. Piney Hollow

10. Barn

11. Small paddock

12. Large fenced-in field

13. Wall jumps

14. Practice obstacle course

15. Pond

16. Fields

17. Hill with view of Shade Valley

Map of the Chambers' Ranch

."Now, Mrs. Bodmer—" began Mr. Chambers.

"When do I get to ride?" Sooze directed her question to Skye.

"Susan, let the man talk!" Mrs. Bodmer snapped. "Be polite for once in your life."

"It's Sooze—S-o-o-z-e—if you don't mind!" she snapped back.

"And what's wrong with your God-given name? You were named after your dear Aunt Susan." Mrs. Bodmer angrily twisted the rings on her fingers. "You just don't like Susan because I do. Plain and simple!"

"I'd rather be named after a circus elephant," Sooze said. She slumped abruptly and stared at the table. "Susan. How *boring!*"

"How did you get the name Sooze?" Mr. Chambers asked in an effort to bring things under control.

"This is *sooo* funny!" Skye giggled and glanced at Sooze. "Go on. Tell him."

Sooze hesitated for a moment, glared at her mother, but finally began to speak. "Chuck, you know my older brother who lives in Kentucky now? He used to let me play in the ashes from our coal furnace when I was real little. He'd laugh his head off and sing, 'Snoozy Sooze, needs a Jacooze.' He'd make me laugh even though I was covered in soot from the top of my head to my little toes. Pretty soon everyone started calling me 'Sooze.' So here I am—Sooze, *not* Susan."

Skye studied Mrs. Bodmer, whose looks soured the room. *And the judge says Sooze is the one who needs help!* Skye thought.

"That's a great story." Mr. Chambers laughed, brushing his straight brown hair back off his forehead. He drew his fingers down both sides of his tidy mustache while he looked first at his wife then at Mrs. Bodmer. "Now, we have some important issues to discuss.

"I've asked Eileen, Skye, and Morgan to meet with us because we have no secrets here." He turned toward the kitchen where the wheelchair-bound girl with long, kinky red hair worked at the sink. "Morgan, would you please join us for a family conference?"

"Coming, Mr. C.," Morgan answered. She closed the dishwasher door before motoring to the gap between Mr. Chambers and Sooze's mother.

"Mrs. Bodmer, this is Morgan Hendricks. She's been with us almost four years now."

"Hi," Morgan said, her freckles dancing with her smile.

"Are you a foster kid too?" Mrs. Bodmer asked.

"Yep," Morgan replied. "And I love it here. This place was made for kids like me. There are ramps and special equipment all over the place. It's so cool."

"Okay—Sooze, we want you to understand exactly why you are here," Mr. Chambers said, folding his hands and looking directly at Sooze. "As you know, your mother feels she is no longer able to control your behavior. She has asked the court to place you in our care. The court ordered that you are to live here as our foster child while you attend the Maranatha Treatment Center program."

"When do I get to ride?" Sooze asked again.

"Susan, will you—" Mrs. Bodmer started sharply.

"Tom," Mrs. Chambers interjected as she stood, "I'll make a pot of coffee. Mrs. Bodmer, would you like some?"

"Yeah," Sooze's mother said, her tone much lighter.

"Girls, how about some iced tea?" Mrs. Chambers asked.

"Sure," Skye and Morgan answered at the same time. Sooze simply nodded.

Mr. Chambers opened a file and shuffled papers, spreading them out before him. "Mrs. Bodmer, according to this court order, Sooze will be with us for at least a year in both the foster home and at Maranatha. We noticed her list of offenses . . . were you aware of her *extracurricular* activities?"

"What do you expect me to do about it!" Mrs. Bodmer said. "It's not like she listens to anything I say."

Everyone expected Sooze to respond to her mother's comment; instead, she leaned forward and placed her hands on each side of her head.

"What's wrong?" Skye whispered. "Another headache?" Sooze nodded.

Mr. Chambers hesitated for a moment as his wife, Eileen, served iced tea to the girls. "Coffee will be ready in a minute," she said.

Mr. Chambers picked up another paper. "Sooze will have counseling at Maranatha three times a week, along with group therapy. Eileen will see that she gets there in the summer. When school starts, Sooze will ride a van with the other clients to the treatment center at three o'clock every afternoon. Then she'll come home with my wife and Skye. Although she won't be living with you for a year, Mrs. Bodmer, we want you to know you are welcome here anytime. Just call before you plan to visit to be sure we're home. Any questions so far?" He put the paper down and folded his hands.

"How much is this going to cost me?" Mrs. Bodmer grumbled.

"Nothing," Mrs. Chambers answered as she placed three cups of coffee on the table. "When a child is court ordered into our program, the expenses are covered by state grants and private donations."

"Good!" Mrs. Bodmer wiped her forehead. "I can't afford anything like this place. I barely make ends meet now, you know, with the house and car payments and all."

"Yeah, and manicures and cigarettes," Sooze threw in.

"Cool it!" Skye jabbed Sooze in the ribs.

As if not hearing Sooze's remark, Mr. Chambers said to her, "Now concerning your responsibilities here. You'll be helping with barn chores, housecleaning, cooking, lawn work—all the skills you will need to manage your own home someday. You'll have your own bedroom. Skye will show it to you in a few minutes. Later, Eileen and I will give you a tour of the barn and introduce you to the horses. From what I've heard, we won't have to hogtie you to get you on a horse. If you're like Skye, I'm sure you'd rather sleep in the barn than in a bed. Anyhow, I would say in about two weeks, you should be adjusted to the daily regimen."

"But it's not all hard work," Morgan added. "We have lots of fun here. It didn't take me long to find out that after the work, there's always time for other things. And we do get five megabucks a week for our chores. Then there's the basement loaded with a pool table, Ping-Pong, and all those video games. And don't forget about the horses!"

"Megabucks—great! And when do I get to ride?" Sooze's words slid out quickly.

Mrs. Bodmer scowled at her daughter. "Susan, you sound like your brain's stuck on *horse, horse, horse*. Can't you get that horse business out of your head? These people are sick of hearing that. Mind your manners, and hush up!"

Skye studied Mrs. Bodmer. *She is so lame.*

"Sooze," Mrs. Chambers said softly, "you'll find out about megabucks soon enough, and you'll get to ride after you've settled in here. We've been discussing which horse would be best for you since you're a beginner, and Skye had a great idea. Tell her, Honey."

"We have six horses, and I figured Stormy, the Tennessee Walker, is one of the gentlest," Skye began.

"Stormy?" Sooze's confusion was apparent. "You have a gentle horse named Stormy?"

"His name matches his color—not the way he acts," Skye said. "His color reminds everyone of a storm cloud. I think he's the one for you."

A smile spread across Sooze's face. "It's no big deal if he's wild or tame. I can ride any kind of horse. Just get me on one, and I'll show you."

Skye rolled her eyes and thought, *Yeah, right!*

"All in good time," Mrs. Chambers said.

"Sooze, you don't just hop on a horse and take off," Morgan added. "Can you believe that I ride even though I can't walk? This cerebral palsy didn't keep me from learning to ride. But it doesn't happen by waving a magic wand. It takes tons of practice."

"You ride horses?" Mrs. Bodmer asked, scratching her head. "How do you get on?"

Mr. Chambers chuckled. "We lift her on, but after that, she's a riding maniac! You should see all her blue ribbons."

"Skye and Champ already have a blue ribbon too!" Morgan said.

"But I practiced a zillion hours before even thinking about a horse show," Skye added.

"Well, sign me up for a blue ribbon," Sooze said. "I can ride too! Just wait and see."

"Susan!" Mrs. Bodmer bellowed. "What am I going to do with her? She never did listen, and it doesn't sound like she's going to start now."

chapter two

Sooze sat cross-legged on her bed with her arms wrapped around Tippy and Tyler, the Chambers' West Highland terriers. "I love horses, I love dogs, and I love this place, Skye."

Skye had plopped onto the same bed with Sooze and now studied the glow on her friend's face.

"This is so cool, Sooze. I mean, you could have been sent to Chesterfield with your record. I think the Chambers put in a good word for you. Even though some of their rules seem stupid, they really do care about us."

"Ever since you invited me to that party a while back, I've been scoping out this place. It is *too* sweet, even with all the rules. I can't wait to get on that horse." Sooze stared, deep in thought. "On the other hand, living here will make it harder until school starts, but I, the Great Sooze, will manage. They do let us out of the cage once in a while, don't they? You know, like, to the mall, or movies, or the store. I have friends all over the place."

Change the subject, Skye told herself. *Get her mind off her old friends.* "We do go to the mall and for groceries every week. You've already seen what that's like

17

when you and Mrs. C. bought stuff for this room." Skye scanned the four walls. "Horse pictures, horse curtains, horse bedspread, horses everywhere! Something tells me you're into horses big time. So you already know we go to the mall. Then there's church."

"Church?" Sooze groaned. "I thought I'd croak when Mr. Chambers mentioned that the other day!"

"I thought no way at first too, but it's really not so bad," Skye said as she leaned against the headboard and clasped her hands behind her head. "The youth-group leader talks about all kinds of neat stuff. Last week he talked about dating. And about how we're not old enough yet."

Skye's thoughts drifted into space as she thought about Chad, who was in the Youth for Truth group, and then she refocused on Sooze. "Besides, Judge Mitchell said you've got to go to church. It won't kill you."

"That's a joke, Skye. I don't need church."

"Hey, I've learned an awful lot living here. One thing I've learned is that I don't need to get in trouble to have a good time. I also don't like to lose control of this." Skye tapped her head. "The last time I did, Mr. C. landed in the hospital. He fell off Chief trying to stop me from taking Champ over a wall jump. If Mr. C. had died, I—I don't know what I'd have done." Skye sighed. "And let me tell you something else. I've been thinking about God."

"I don't want to hear it."

"No—wait! Listen, I used to think God didn't exist until he healed Mr. C. from that head injury. At least I think he did. Now I'm thinking twice about this God stuff. Sooze, he *might* be real!"

"Yeah, and turtles *might* do back flips. What's going on with you? You used to be so much fun, but I've seen you change in the last few months. Are they getting to you?"

"Nobody's *getting* to me, Sooze. I've just been trying to *get* my act together. I used to be so mad at my parents, whoever and wherever they are, that I was always angry.

18

Maybe that's part of your problem too. You're mad at the whole world."

"Don't put your stuff off on me, Skye." Sooze scrunched up her face. "The only people I'm mad at are my so-called mother and those know-it-all teachers at school. Truth is, I don't care about nothing anymore. But this idea of yours—it sounded like fun, so I figured why not? And then the way it turned out—living here—that's even better. Why not be as close to the horses—and dogs—as possible?" She kissed the dogs and hugged them tighter.

"You don't know the Chambers like I do," Skye said. "They have eyes in the back of their heads. You are *not* going to get away with anything here. Trust me on this one."

"Watch me!" Sooze hissed.

"Yeah, I'll watch you being grounded like I was for breaking the rules. Then there's the biggest pain of all—no horse, no barn, nothing. It stinks. Believe me, I know!"

"What about all our barn chores that we absolutely have to do every day? Huh? What then? Huh? You can touch the horses then, can't you?" Sooze raised her eyebrows.

"Somebody else does your chores, even if it means Mr. or Mrs. C. They will *not* let you near that barn if you get grounded. You might as well be in jail."

"I guess I'll have to make sure I don't get caught," Sooze said, her face beaming with a devilish smile.

"Can I join the party?" Morgan said, as she motored up to the doorway. "Mrs. C. wants to feed Tip and Ty. Okay, guys. Lunch is served!"

As the dogs jumped from the bed and made a hasty exit, Skye looked Morgan's way and smiled. *Whew, am I glad you're here,* her face said.

Sooze's eyes lit up with surprise. "Hey, how did the dogs know their food was ready?"

"Those dogs listen better than we do," Skye said.

"All you have to do is say the word *lunch*, and they're history," Morgan said as she moved next to the bed.

"Hey, Morgan, get this," Skye said. "Sooze thinks she's going to run her own show here. Want to tell her different?"

"You are in for the surprise of your life," Morgan said, flipping back her red hair. "I remember how clueless I was when I moved in. But I figured it out soon enough. Grounding. Grounding. And more grounding. I thought I'd never see the outside world again."

Sooze sprawled out across the bed on her belly. "How do you get grounded when you're already *grounded* in that thing? It's not like you're going to be running away or stealing a car or anything!"

"Hey, I can drive! I drive a special van the Chambers have. I just got my license." Morgan said as she flicked her head with a bit of pride. "But I wouldn't think of doing anything as lame as stealing the van. The Chambers have been too good to me. And besides, it's just plain stupid. Being grounded is awful. You lose phone and computer privileges, and I love playing Battleship on the Internet." Morgan flipped the joystick on her wheelchair, sending her chair into a slow rotation. "And as far as this *thing*, it's called a Jazzy, and it can do just about anything but fly. See?"

"That's pretty cool!" Sooze said with a patronizing smile. Then she put her hands on the sides of her head and dug her elbows into the bed.

"Another headache?" Skye asked.

"Yeah," Sooze groaned.

"Headaches?" Morgan brought her chair to a stop. "You ought to tell Mrs. C. Sounds like you need your head examined."

"Yeah, it's probably empty!" Skye giggled.

Sooze blinked her eyes a couple of times. "Mom says it's from me spending so much time freaking out. She says I'm a walking time bomb and when the headaches stop, I'll explode. So you two better cross your fingers and hope this thumping doesn't stop, or the whole place will be Soozified!" She giggled weakly and pressed her head tighter.

Skye raised both hands, fingers crossed.

"Hey, I know what we can do," Morgan said. She started to back out of the room. "We can all pray about it."

"Pray? Don't think so," Sooze snapped. "That won't do any good."

Skye could tell her friend was in real pain. She promised herself to tell Mrs. C. about it.

"When do I get to ride?" Sooze asked Skye as they leaned up against the white fence that bordered the pasture. To their right, a poor excuse for a truck, loaded with hay, rattled down the dirt road. The hot July sun washed over the girls' faces, forcing them to shield their eyes with their hands.

"You know, Sooze, your mom might not be right about a lot of things, but she's right on about you having your brain stuck on *horses*," Skye said. "You've only been here for two days. I'm sure Mr. and Mrs. C. have big plans for you today. But I think I know what's coming first."

"Hey, I already know plenty about riding horses," Sooze protested. "I've ridden lots of times at carnivals, and I even went to a riding camp once. I got my way paid on some kind of grant through the school. I always rode this one neat pony, Sugar. We'd go around and around in the corral until they made me get off."

"Riding a pony in a corral or in a circle at a carnival is so *not* the same as riding well-trained registered horses like these," Skye said. "Stormy knows what to do in an open field, but do you?"

"Don't get all preachy," Sooze said. "I know what I'm doing. You'll see."

"Yeah, you'll see," Skye snickered. "I bet you have a lot to learn."

"Hey, you two," Mr. Chambers yelled as he got out of the truck, slamming the squeaky door shut. "Let's get this hay loaded into the loft. Then we'll show Sooze more of her chores in the barn!" Mr. Chambers grinned slyly.

"Great," Sooze complained. "I can hardly wait."

"Yeah, they're nasty," Skye said, "especially mucking out the stalls. But at least we're close to the horses. Come on. Let's do the hay-into-the-loft thing. Then I'm sure Mr. C. will saddle up the horses."

"What's mucking?" Sooze asked suspiciously.

"You'll see soon enough," Skye answered with a grin.

For the next half hour, Mr. Chambers pitched hay bales from the truck to Skye and Sooze in the loft of the barn. The girls dragged one bale at a time into the back and pushed and pulled each one onto a huge stack that looked like gigantic toy blocks against the wall. Covered with hay shreds and dust, they finally placed the last bale and then hurried to join Mr. Chambers on the ground level at the horse stalls.

"Good job, girls," Mr. Chambers said, dusting himself off with his stained, tan cowboy hat. "Maybe the next time you should wear long sleeves and jeans like I suggested." His mustache chuckled. "Hay dust makes you very itchy."

Maybe I like to itch! Skye thought to herself. "Too hot for jeans," she said matter-of-factly.

"Well, at least you have your boots on, Skye. I guess you know what's coming."

"Yeah, I know," Skye said, grinning.

"Sooze, you need a good pair of cowboy boots," Mr. Chambers added. "But until we take you shopping, I don't want you to ruin your sneakers."

This ought to be good, Skye laughed to herself. "Sooze, over there against the wall are a couple of pairs of big rubber boots. Pick the right size and put them on over your shoes."

"What do I need them for? It's not snowing," Sooze complained as she walked to the wall.

"No, but you'll wish it was when you see what we're getting ready to do," Skye said.

"Skye," Mr. Chambers said, walking away, "since Stormy is going to be Sooze's horse, how about you two start with that stall? I'll work the other side of the barn."

"Right, Mr. C.," Skye said as she pointed. "Sooze, get the pitchfork and shovel down from the wall hooks. I'll get the wheelbarrow, and a-mucking we will go."

"I'm getting a bad feeling about this," Sooze said, starting toward the boots.

"Come on. You'll love it!" Skye said, smiling. "Mucking is the only gross part of this horse stuff. Every day we have to shovel you-know-what out of each stall. But it doesn't take long to become a champion pooper-scooper. Really, it's not that bad, especially when you love horses. It just gives us another chance to be near them. And this is super important."

Skye opened Stormy's stall and continued her instructions. "After mucking, we put a fresh layer of straw down every day. It's not only easier on this," she said, pointing to her nose, "but it's mega-important for the horses' hooves. If they get thrush from standing in this stuff for days, they can go lame. Thrush is an infection that eats away the bottom of their hooves. And it smells worse than a garbage can on a hot summer day. So we *have to* do this. Got it?"

"Got it," Sooze said as she crumpled up her face and held her nose. "When do I get to ride?"

"Tomorrow!" Mr. Chambers yelled from the other end of the barn. "After you get your boots."

chapter three

Sooze, you look like you're ready to jump out of your skin!" Skye said from outside the training corral next to the barn. Skye was sitting on Champ, and his sorrel coat was gleaming in the sun. "It's finally your turn. Hey, where'd you get those jeans and fancy boots and that hard hat?"

"Yeah," Morgan said. "Looks like you're ready to go in the house and do some dishes." She positioned Blaze, her Quarter Horse mare, next to Champ.

"Very funny," Sooze said as she sat on the corral rail, waiting for Mr. Chambers to bring Stormy out of the barn. She fooled with the hard hat, trying to get it to balance on her head. "I don't need this dumb thing."

"Girls, girls, have mercy on this poor child," Mrs. Chambers said as she walked next to Sooze and gently touched her on the back. "Sooze, you have to wear the hat. State regulations."

Sooze shrugged off Mrs. Chambers' hand.

I remember when I pulled away from Mrs. Chambers like that, Skye told herself. *Sooze, you don't know what you're missing—a mother's real love.* "Sooze can take anything we dish out. She's t-o-u-g-h with a capital T. Aren't you, Sooze?"

Skye studied Sooze, waiting for a response, but Sooze was focused on the barn. One of the doors slid open, and all eyes shifted.

Mr. Chambers walked out of the barn leading a charcoal gray horse with a long, flowing mane and tail. The horse, dressed in a royal-blue blanket and tan western saddle and bridle, glistened in the sun. Skye gazed at the gorgeous creature, recalling the one time she rode Stormy.

"He's too big for me," Skye said to Champ as she patted him on the neck, "but you're just right, boy."

"Stormy is a big guy," Morgan said, "but he's as gentle as he is big. He ought to be a good match for Sooze."

"It's not Sooze I'm worried about," Skye said. "I don't think Stormy knows what *he's* in for. We might see him freak out for the first time in his life when Supergirl gets on him."

"Hey, watch it," Sooze answered back.

"Okay, Sooze," Mr. Chambers said as he led Stormy into the corral and closed the gate. "You've mastered your grooming, saddling, and leading sessions. Now it's time for you to mount."

Sooze wasted no time jumping down off the fence and running toward the horse. "Finally!" she yelled, hard hat wobbling and new boots causing her to stumble.

"Whoa, slow down!" Mr. Chambers said. "You don't want to spook him. Remember, I told you to approach a horse—any horse—cautiously. Now stroke his neck and let him see you. Talk to him—softly. Let him smell you, so he can prepare himself for 'The Great Sooze.'"

"Sooze, you sure you wouldn't rather be cleaning your room?" Skye laughed, and Morgan joined in.

"Girls, stop it," Mrs. Chambers gently chided. "You're wasting your breath. Just sit back and enjoy the ride."

"One thing about Sooze," Skye said, "she's no chicken like I was on my first ride. I don't think she's afraid of anything."

"Hmm," Mrs. Chambers said. "That's not always good, especially when you're around such powerful animals."

"Hopefully, living here will help her get her act together," Morgan said. "At school she's on the Top Ten list of the wildest kids at Madison. Mrs. C., I think you've got an impossible mission with this one."

"Well, with God's help, we can and will help her. Mr. C. and I are praying for her, just like we prayed for both of you."

Yeah, Skye thought. *We'll see.*

"Up you go!" With a strong shoulder, Mr. Chambers boosted Sooze onto the patient horse. Sooze leveled her wobbly hat while Mr. Chambers checked the length of each stirrup. "Now take the reins in one hand, and I'm going to hold on to the bridle. We'll walk around in this corral until you feel 'tall in the saddle,' as they say. Maybe in a week or two you'll be able to take him out in the open field."

Sooze confidently adjusted her hard hat. "I can do that now. I know what to do. I've ridden lots a times."

"Sooze, tune in to Mr. C!" Skye yelled from the sidelines. "He knows what he's talking about."

"Patience, Sooze," Mrs. Chambers added. "Patience."

"But I've done this before," Sooze whined.

Mr. Chambers walked to the front of the horse and held the bridle. "Sooze, now listen to me. You have *never* ridden a horse like this one. Believe me. This is a Tennessee Walking Horse. You have to know what you're doing to, let's say, make him *work* right. God made this breed different from all others."

Skye scrunched up her face. She could tell Sooze didn't want to hear it.

"Sooze, why do you think he's called a Tennessee Walker?" Mr. Chambers asked.

"Because he's too lazy to run!" she retorted. "Let's go!"

"No, we're going to wait until you calm down. A horse can read you like a book, even before you get on his back. As wired as you are, Stormy might give you a ride into the next county. Now just stroke his neck and release the reins while I tell you about Walkers. This is part of your training."

"Oh, fine." Sooze pouted.

Mr. Chambers began. "Walkers don't trot, nor do they run like other horses. God gave them a running walk. Their diagonal legs work almost in unison, all four hitting the ground at a different time, maybe a second apart. Their back legs have tremendous overstride, which causes an even rocking-horse action when they speed up. Now, you won't feel that when Stormy walks slowly, but as soon as you squeeze your legs the right way, he will be off into the smoothest ride you've ever felt—as smooth as running water. You'll feel like you're riding on a cloud. But first, you have to learn how to get onboard. You are sitting on a blue-ribbon show horse, Sooze. Don't forget that."

"I won't. Let's go!"

"All right. Now we're going to walk slowly in this ring for a long time. I'll show you how to stop, turn, and back up, and you can practice mounting and dismounting. Even though he's over sixteen hands, once you can get your foot in the stirrup with ease, I think you'll be mounting without help from anyone. Ready?"

"Yes!"

"Here we go," Mr. Chambers said. He stepped to the left side of Stormy and clicked his tongue.

"Ride 'em cowgirl!" Mrs. Chambers yelled.

"Hey, Sooze, the dishes are waiting!" Morgan joked.

"Good-bye, carnival ponies. Hello, Stormy!" Skye added.

Sooze's face glowed with delight as the trio circled the corral. Skye couldn't remember seeing her friend so happy in all the time they'd known each other.

Skye sat in the dining room with Morgan and the Chambers during lunch break. Like a beaver chewing a log, Skye ate a row of corn on the cob then asked: "Mrs. C., could we go to the mall one day this week? I've got my eye on a new video game."

"Oh," Mrs. Chambers replied, "I thought you said last week you needed new shoes for church and special occasions."

"Nah, the shoes can wait. I've got to have this game. Can we go?"

Mr. Chambers swallowed a bite of his sandwich. "Now, Skye, don't you think you should budget some of your allowance for important things—like a pair of shoes? I just realized that lately we haven't discussed giving to the Lord. Have you been tithing? You haven't forgotten about giving that ten percent, have you?"

I know God is real, but I'm sure he doesn't need my measly couple of bucks! A faint smile disguised Skye's thoughts.

"No, I didn't forget," she murmured.

"Good," Mrs. Chambers said. "Don't leave the Lord out of any part of your life, Honey."

"I remember how hard it was for me to get into the habit of giving my tithe at first," Morgan said as she munched a potato chip. "But when I learned how God uses what we give to help others, I finally got into it. It's so cool to see how my money can be used to help missionaries or families in need. I get as much out of giving as those getting the help. And God promises special blessings to those who tithe. I read about it in the book of Malachi, in the Bible. You'll see."

Want to bet? Skye thought. "Whatever," she mumbled.

Mr. Chambers finished his glass of water and wiped his mustache. "Hey, where did Sooze go? She's been gone quite awhile, and she hasn't finished her lunch."

"She said she had to use the bathroom," Mrs. Chambers said. "Skye, would you mind checking on her?"

"No problem."

Skye pushed back her chair and headed down the hallway, knocking on the bathroom door. There was no answer, so Skye knocked again. Finally, she peeked in. The bathroom was empty, and the window was wide open!

"Mrs. C!" Skye yelled. "Sooze isn't in the bathroom, and the window's open!" Skye called out, running back into the dining room.

Morgan had just pivoted her chair to glance out the sliding glass doors. "Hey—how did Stormy get out into the big field?"

Everyone turned to the window in time to see Sooze trying to mount from the far side.

Mr. and Mrs. Chambers jumped up from the table so fast they almost toppled their chairs as they ran for the door. Skye was right behind them.

"And no hard hat!" Mr. Chambers bellowed. He opened the door in one swift move and charged out. "Sooze, don't get on that horse!"

"She'll kill herself!" Mrs. Chambers said.

Skye ran toward the field with Morgan motoring along behind her.

As Mr. Chambers raced across the lawn, Stormy pranced in tight circles with Sooze already on his back.

"Watch me now!" she yelled. "I'll show you I can ride!"

Mr. Chambers took one courageous leap toward the fence. "Sooze, stop!"

Stormy wheeled, and Sooze grabbed the horn with one hand and the reins with the other. She shoved her heels into the unsuspecting horse's belly. Hard.

"You idiot!" Skye screamed, running to the fence. "That's no play pony!"

"Sooze! Sooze!" Mrs. Chambers, out of breath at the fence, could not utter another word.

"Sooze!" Morgan yelled. "Stop!"

"Let's go, Stormy!" Sooze whooped. "Let's show 'em how it's done!"

chapter four

Every muscle in Stormy's powerful body tensed with the excitement of running like the wind. A kick that hard in such well-trained ribs meant only one thing: Go fast!

In a split second, Stormy broke into a fast gallop and tore along the fence with Sooze hanging on for dear life. Like a rag doll tied to the saddle, she bounced with every hoof beat that pounded the ground. Pulling back hard on the reins, she screamed, "Whoa! Whoa!"

As Sooze flew by, Mr. Chambers, balancing on the fence railings, reached out for her but just missed her. "Turn him in a circle!" he yelled as he cleared the fence and ran after Stormy.

"Sooze!" Skye and Morgan yelled together, eyes wide with alarm. "Turn him in a circle!"

Stormy rounded the corner, charging toward the bottom of the field. As he scraped against the fence on the turn, Sooze leaned over to her right and managed to wrap her arms around a fence post. Stormy continued racing down the field at full speed, leaving his rider dangling. Sooze dropped to the ground, badly shaken but unharmed.

Mr. Chambers joined Sooze, steadying her shoulders before looking into her eyes. "Are you all right?"

"What on earth were you trying to do?" Mrs. Chambers puffed as she and Skye approached.

"That was dumb!" Skye panted. "You could've killed yourself!" *And who else pulled a stupid stunt like that on a horse not too long ago?* immediately popped into in Skye's mind.

"Stupid horse!" Sooze complained as she glared at Stormy, who was now munching grass down near the pond. "It wasn't my fault. Something spooked him."

"Yeah, right," Skye retorted. "I think the spook was on his back."

For the rest of the afternoon at Keystone Stables, the mood was somber and tense. Sooze's disobedience put pleasure on the back burner, but the business of running a ranch took over. While Mr. Chambers cut hay on the lower fields, Mrs. Chambers and the girls blanched twenty dozen ears of corn, bagged them, and stored them in one of the basement freezers.

While Sooze sulked and complained about the work, Skye and Morgan tried to eat as much corn as they bagged. They told silly jokes, determined to change Mrs. Chambers' disgruntled mood.

"Man, is Mrs. C. ticked." Skye whispered to Sooze over a boiling pot of corn. "You are going to get it. Big time!"

"Watch me!" was Sooze's smart reply.

The mood at supper was somewhat lighter, however. (If they had been practicing to eat politely before the Queen of England, everyone would have passed with flying colors.) Mr. Chambers reviewed the next week's activities, and Mrs. Chambers talked about a shopping trip. After supper, the family met in the living room for devotions and a family discussion.

"Just remember, girls," Mr. Chambers said as he glanced up from his Bible, "you can't earn your way to heaven. In the book of Ephesians it says that eternal life is a result of God's grace—his undeserved favor. It's a gift you can't see but you can receive by faith. All you need to do is believe that Jesus Christ died and rose again for your sins and ask him to forgive you."

Skye fixed her gaze on a vase of flowers on the end table beside Mr. Chambers.

"My life has never been the same since I did that many years ago," Mrs. Chambers added. "Girls, God gives you a peace in your heart that's hard to understand."

Morgan smiled and directed her words at Skye and Sooze. "I accepted Christ as my Savior after I moved in here, and it's so cool having the Lord as my best friend. He's always there to help me through tough times. Now I finally have my head screwed on straight instead of making stupid choices that get me in trouble."

Skye stared at the floor and couldn't help but notice that Sooze was doing the same thing.

"The Lord does help us with our decisions, girls." Mr. Chambers laid down his Bible. "Eileen and I pray daily that we will lead you girls down the right cow path," he added with a smirk in a show of his returning humor. "Right now we need to discuss what happened earlier today with Stormy. Sooze, since you disobeyed in front of the whole family, everyone is included in this discussion. We value all of your opinions on decisions we must make. We want you to tell us how you see things."

"It wasn't my fault," Sooze snapped. "I told you I know how to ride."

"She has been to riding camps a couple of times, Mr. C.," Skye added in support.

"Skye," Mrs. Chambers leaned forward on the sofa, "you know our horses are not like camp horses and ponies. We've warned you all well in advance how much training it takes to handle one of these show horses. It's a big deal. We're talking about your safety and the horse's safety, not to mention thousands of dollars."

Mr. Chambers sat back rigidly in his chair with his elbows on the armrests, one finger absently stroking his mustache. "Sooze, I'm afraid you've broken the all-time record for the kid to get grounded the quickest after moving in. If it were a lesser offense, we might go a little easier. But we just cannot tolerate reckless behavior around the horses. Somebody could get killed."

"But I told you it wasn't my fault!" Sooze whined, slumping in her chair.

You better cool it, Skye thought, *or they'll tack on another week for griping.* Skye caught Sooze's eye and shook her head in silent warning.

Mr. Chambers spelled out the sentence. "Young lady, you will be grounded for two weeks. No mall, no trips, no recreation room, no phone. You will still be expected to do your household chores and yard work, but the barn and the horses are off limits. The rest of us will cover your chores down there.

"Skye and Morgan may still visit you in your room each night for a half hour, and you will still go with us to church. Other than that, life will be crawling a little slowly for you. Now, you don't have to lock yourself up in your room. You are not in jail. We want you at every meal and in all the family devotions and discussions. But your other activities will have to wait."

"That's so not fair!" Sooze griped. "You're not giving me a chance. I hate this place!"

"Sooze," Morgan said, "why don't you give us a chance—and this place?"

"We love you and want you here with us," Mrs. Chambers said. "But you have to cooperate."

"All your rules are stupid," Sooze said. "My mother doesn't make me do anything. I can do whatever I want!"

"Does that make you happy, Sooze?" Mrs. Chambers asked.

"When I get what I want—which is most of the time," Sooze answered smartly.

"Can't you give her another chance?" Skye pleaded, turning to face Mr. Chambers.

"Oh, but we are," Mr. Chambers reasoned. "She's getting the same chance as you and Morgan. We're trying to help you girls learn what's most important in life. Sooze, you'll get nowhere thinking everything that happens to you is someone else's fault. We're praying that you accept this discipline and learn from it. You may go to your room. Morgan and Skye may visit you later for a while if they'd like. And remember," he said, "we're doing this to help you, not to hurt you."

"Yeah, right," Sooze replied sarcastically.

Sooze hurried out of the room and ran down the hall. She slammed her bedroom door so hard it shook the whole house.

Uh, oh. I smell trouble, Skye thought. Almost getting bucked from Stormy was going to be the least of Sooze's complaints.

Before bedtime, Skye knocked on Sooze's door with Morgan trailing right behind.

"Hey, what's up?" Skye asked, as she gently pushed open the door.

"Nothing. Just go away and leave me alone!" Sooze fumed, leaning up against the headboard and planting her sneakers firmly on the bed. She pressed her head with her hands. Obvious pain shrouded her face.

"No problem," Morgan said, pivoting and heading out the doorway. "I have better things to do than listen to this baloney."

"Another headache?" Skye asked as she turned toward the door. "No wonder you're in such a lousy mood. I'll see you in the morning."

"No—wait," Sooze whispered. "C'mere."

"I wish you'd make up your mind. What's up?" Skye asked as she sat on the edge of the bed.

Sooze ignored the question, sliding next to Skye, "I'm out of here tonight. Are you with me?"

"Are you crazy?" Skye whispered loudly. "Where would you go? And how? Sooze, think! This might land you in Chesterfield for good, and you'll never get to ride Stormy again."

"Well, big deal!" Sooze growled. "What's the difference? They are not going to tell me what to do—here or anyplace else."

"Where are you going? And how?"

"Skye, sometimes you are as thick as that wall. The Chambers have a piece of junk with four wheels they call a truck. Right?"

"Yeah—so?"

"I'm taking that truck, and I'm history. I've watched every time Mr. C. has parked it, and he always throws the keys under the seat. So, are you coming with me or not?"

Skye chewed her lip, trying not to let her face show her fear. "Sooze, this is so not a good idea. You can't drive. You're only fourteen."

"Hey, been there, done that. There's nothing to it," Sooze said smugly. "I'm only asking you one more time. Are you coming or not?"

"Where to? And for how long? Where will you stay? How will you eat?"

"I told you I have friends all over the place. Some of them live just an hour from here. They'll hide us until I can think this through. I don't need this goody-two-shoes life."

"I—I don't know. It sounds really stupid to me."

"Fine," Sooze mocked. "If you never want to see me again, that's fine. But if you want to help me, meet me down at the truck at midnight."

Skye pulled the curtain back on her bedroom window. The clear night sky twinkled with a curtain of stars, and a full moon lit up everything outside with a soft white glow. She studied the backyard intently, focusing on a figure creeping down to the barn and slipping into the front seat of the old pickup. Skye lifted her window an inch and listened to the engine grinding. With headlights out, the truck crawled along the dirt road from the side of the barn, past the house, and onto the main road. There it sat idling.

Sooze, you are so dead! Skye couldn't let her go like this. She inched her window up a couple of feet, slid out quietly, and darted across the lawn. Panting, she reached the road and ran around to the door on the passenger side of the truck. Carefully, she squeaked it open and slid in.

"So you're not so chicken after all," Sooze whispered. She pulled the knob for the lights, jammed the gearshift into drive, and crept down the road away from Keystone Stables.

"Sooze, this is so not the way to do this," Skye said. "Maybe you can be placed in a different foster home if you hate it here so much."

"I am so sick of people telling me what to do!" Sooze's voice rose in anger as the truck's speed increased. "I have had it up to here with rules." She lifted her hand and made a slicing motion across her neck.

In an instant, with only one inexperienced hand on its steering wheel, Sooze jerked the truck and the tires caught on the gravel shoulder of the narrow road. The truck spun out of control

Skye's body jolted against the door. As she righted herself, her eyes fixed on a fast approaching horseshoe turn.

"Look out!" Skye screamed in horror. "You're going too fast! Slow down!"

Sooze fought the wheel to steady the truck, which was now completely out of control.

"Oh no!" Skye screamed. And then everything went black.

chapter five

Skye lay on a hospital bed with a gauze patch taped above one eyebrow. Scrapes and bruises covered her body. She ached as though she had been twisted into a pretzel and tied up for days.

What happened? Where am I? she wondered. Then it all came flooding back. Groaning, she finally managed to turn her head just enough to see a clock on the wall.

Three o'clock! It's been hours.

Time to think often found itself on the bottom of Skye's priority list. Thinking left her feeling depressed and alone, even in the middle of a cheering crowd at the Madison football games. But now, for the first time in her short, thirteen-year life, Skye allowed herself to consider what could have happened, and she felt terribly alone.

God, thank you for sending someone to help us. Skye gasped a sudden breath. *Did I just thank God for saving me? The God I have no time for? What if I'd died? What if this had been my last day on Earth?* Skye wondered. *What would I have to show God, so he would let me into heaven?*

"Nothing," Skye whispered out loud. "Nothing but a rotten attitude and a record of trouble as long as my arm."

A flood of tears drenched her cheeks, and an overwhelming sense of guilt flooded her soul.

God would never want me! she thought. *I'm too rotten!*

Then it was as if Mr. Chambers was standing right beside her. She remembered what he'd said to them: "You can't earn your way to heaven. It's God's gift. Just ask him to forgive you of your sins, and you'll be a new person, inside and out!"

Then Skye remembered Morgan's words: "Jesus is the best friend I have. He's always there when I need him."

I need you right now, God! Skye's heart cried out.

Just then, a pretty nurse with dark hair and kind eyes came through the doors. "So you're awake, are you?" she said. "As soon as the doctor checks you out, some people here are anxious to see you."

Again, the doors opened, and a man in a white lab coat, with straight black hair, hurried in. Reading glasses were perched on his nose as he glanced at a clipboard.

"Skye Nicholson," he said, flipping through some papers. "I'm Dr. Wang. You are one fortunate young lady. You and your friend both hit your heads on the windshield. It seems that someone's been watching out for you," he said as he gently examined Skye's head, neck, and shoulders.

The doctor nodded at the nurse, who walked to the door and waved. Mrs. Chambers rushed into the room with her husband following close behind.

"Honey, are you all right?" Mrs. Chambers asked.

"You sure know how to scare the wits out of us," Mr. Chambers said, forcing a smile. "What were you two trying to do?"

"Where's Sooze? Is she okay?" Skye rubbed her swollen, tear-soaked eyes.

"Sooze is in another room," Mr. Chambers said. "She's got a nasty bump on her head. She's still a little dizzy, but the doctor thinks she'll be okay. It's a miracle you two weren't seriously injured—or killed! The truck is totaled, but God had his hand of protection on you two. No doubt about it."

"When will she be released?" Mrs. Chambers asked.

"We need to keep her for observation. You can probably take her home tomorrow. However," Dr. Wang directed his words back to Skye, "you take it easy for a few days. You've got some serious bruising, and those stitches above your eye need time to heal. No cartwheels or jumping out of airplanes or anything. Okay?"

"What about Sooze—Susan Bodmer—across the hall?" Mrs. Chambers asked. "May we take her with us too?"

Dr. Wang looked through another set of papers. "Hmm," he said, deep in thought. "Preliminary skull X-rays show something that we'd like to examine a little further. She got a nasty bump on the left side of her head. We'd like to keep her a few more days for observation and run more tests. It's probably nothing, but we want to make sure. She's complaining of a severe headache."

"Sooze has a lot of headaches," Skye said.

Mrs. Chambers' face reflected deep concern. "She's been our foster child for less than a week. She hasn't told us about the headaches, and her health records show no such problem."

"Like I said," Dr. Wang replied, "it's probably nothing, but I would like our neurosurgeon to take a look at the test results. We're going to move her upstairs now. If you wait a little longer, you should be able to see her."

"Yes, we'll wait," Mr. Chambers said. "We'll go grab coffee and wait in Skye's room."

"The nurse will let you know when you can see Susan," Dr. Wang said. "She'll direct you to Susan's room. I'm sure she'll be very glad to see you."

In the dimly lit hospital room, Skye sipped chocolate milk from a carton while Mr. and Mrs. Chambers drank coffee from Styrofoam cups like two robots. All three struggled with heavy eyelids.

Mrs. Chambers broke the hush. "This place makes you want to whisper, doesn't it?"

"Yeah," Mr. Chambers said. Finishing his coffee, he stared at Skye. "How do you feel?"

"Okay," she said. "Just a little stiff is all."

Mrs. Chambers sipped her coffee. "Where did you girls think you were going at that hour? And what made you two think Sooze could drive a truck?"

Skye set down her carton. "You probably won't believe me, but I was trying to stop her. She wanted to drive to some friend's house about an hour from here. I went with her to try to talk her out of it. I know I could've been killed!"

Skye felt her face flush. Tears streamed down her face and onto her hospital gown.

"What's the matter, Honey?" Mrs. Chambers gently rubbed Skye's back and handed her a tissue.

"I'm just so sorry," was all Skye could manage between sobs.

"We know you are," Mr. Chambers said. "There will be some consequences later, but for now we want you to know that we still love you."

"I don't mean just this," Skye said, rubbing her tear-filled eyes. "I mean I'm sorry for everything. Mr. C., I've been thinking about what you said in devotions the other night—you know, about God's gift? I want to ask Jesus to forgive me and save me. Would I have to wait until church on Sunday to do that?"

Mr. Chambers' face broke into a smile. "Skye, that's the best news ever. We've been praying every day that you would feel the need to turn your life over to God. And no, you don't need to wait until Sunday. You can do it right here—right now."

"What do I do?" Skye asked.

Mrs. Chambers reached over and took Skye's hand.

"We can pray together right here," Mr. Chambers responded. "Remember what we've said about God being so holy that sin can't exist in his presence? As a righteous judge, the sentence he requires for sin and rebellion is death. But as soon as the sentence was announced, God asked his own son, Jesus Christ, to die on the cross in your place. And that's exactly what he did. Jesus wasn't guilty of anything, but he took all the sin of the world, including everything you've ever done wrong, and died for you so that you wouldn't have to."

Skye couldn't believe what she was hearing. "You mean, I should have gotten the death penalty, but Jesus took it for me? I don't understand. Why would he do that?"

"He did that because he loves you, Skye, more than you will ever fully know. Tell you what," Mr. Chambers said, placing his cup on a table, "let's pray right now. God doesn't expect any fancy words, Skye. All he wants to know is that you want to accept his wonderful gift and receive forgiveness."

Folding her hands, Skye bowed her head. Different from all the other times she had prayed, she closed her eyes, concentrating on Jesus, the one who had always loved her in spite of her faults.

"Dear God," she said, "I know I've been rotten, and I don't blame you if you're mad at me. But if it's true that you want to forgive me, I'm asking you to do that right now. I'm sorry for everything I've ever done wrong. Jesus, thank you for taking my sin on yourself so I can be forgiven and go to heaven. Amen."

Skye glanced at the only two people who had ever shown real care and concern for her. She couldn't contain her smile as she reflected on what she had just done.

"Skye," Mrs. Chambers said, eyes sparkling with joy, "we love you so much."

"Yes, we do," Mr. Chambers added, "and according to the Bible, God does too. Now, young lady, you are part of another family—the family of God."

Skye took in a deep breath of air, but the bruises that made it painful to breathe. It didn't matter how she felt on the outside, though, because, for the first time in her life, Skye felt really clean on the inside. At last, she was free from the anger and hatred that had weighed her down. Now she was free to love, starting with the two greatest people she had ever known.

"And I love you both—Mom and Dad."

chapter six

A t home, Skye focused on her nightstand clock and
shot upright in bed. Pain flashed through her body,
even though one whole day had passed since the
accident.

"Ten o'clock! Ow! Oh—oh," she groaned and fell back
on her pillow. Then she remembered. The accident—the
hospital—the cut above her eye—the bruises. No wonder she felt like she'd been run over by a truck!

Skye struggled to roll over to sit on the edge of her
bed and caught a glimpse of herself in the dresser mirror.
Yikes! she thought.

Skye unfolded herself, one sore limb at a time, and
struggled to stand. *It's cool that the Chambers let me
sleep in. I wonder how Sooze is doing?*

Despite the bruises on the outside, Skye felt as though
a cool stream flowed through her soul, bringing peace.
Now she could face the morning with a smile, one that
came from the depths of her new spirit. She couldn't get
over how different she felt—new. She limped to her window and looked out.

The day was already a muggy, overcast gray, but even the weather couldn't dampen the sunshine Skye felt inside. Something special *had* happened! Like a dirty stable made clean, her own heart had been "mucked out." This was the second day of her new, sparkling-clean life with God. The Chambers had kept her in bed and quiet after she got home from the hospital the day before, but today she would be able to talk to Morgan. She could hardly wait to tell her the good news.

Despite her pain, Skye hurried to dress and brush her hair. She hobbled out of her bedroom and made her way down the hallway into the dining room. The welcoming fragrance of coffee and buttered toast greeted her along with Mr. and Mrs. Chambers.

The couple sat close to one another, enjoying a late breakfast. The dogs, Tip and Ty, crouched under the table, stalking any handouts that might come their way.

"Did Mary Brannigan call you?" Mrs. Chambers asked her husband. "Her computer froze, and she thinks her hard drive crashed. I saw her at the market yesterday."

"No, not yet. I hope she does though. I can always use the business." Mr. Chambers then directed his attention to Skye. "Well, good morning, and where do you think you're going?"

Mrs. Chambers swallowed a bite of toast. "Honey, you can't possibly do chores today. We're going to do them for you. Oh my, just look at your poor face!"

"Where's Morgan?" Skye said as she leaned against the table. "You didn't tell her, did you? Where is she?"

"Whoa, take it easy, girl. She's down at the barn," Mr. Chambers said, eating the last of his scrambled eggs.

"And yes, we told her about the accident," Mrs. Chambers added, sipping her coffee.

"No, no, I don't mean about the accident. I mean about me—and God—what happened at the hospital."

"No, we didn't tell her," Mrs. Chambers said. "We figured you'd want to tell her all about that yourself. Now sit down and have some breakfast."

"But I want to tell her right now. Can I? Please? Then I'll eat."

"Sure," Mr. Chambers grinned. "The decision you made to accept Christ was the most important one you'll ever make. Go on."

Mrs. Chambers smiled. "I'll keep the eggs warm in the microwave. Now go ahead before you forget what happened." Both she and Mr. Chambers laughed.

Skye hobbled down to the barn as fast as her aching legs would go. She squeezed through the sliding door and hurried past every stall. Frustrated, she finally yelled, "Morgan!"

"In the tack room!" Morgan yelled back.

Skye hurried to the small room decked with saddles and bridles hanging on the walls. The pungent aromas of leather, horses, and hay saturated the air. Morgan sat in the center of the room, polishing a saddle mounted on a sawhorse.

"Hey, sleepyhead! You're finally among the land of the living!" Morgan kidded and then looked up. Her green eyes gawked in disbelief. "No way! Look at those black eyes! What were you two trying to prove?"

Skye limped to the center of the room. Overturning an old bucket, she placed her aching body gingerly in front of Morgan, who went back to soaping the saddle.

"You know the fair is only a month away," Morgan started. "We have tons of work to do before—"

"Morgan, I've gotta tell you something," Skye interrupted.

"If it's about the accident and Sooze, I already know. Mr. and Mrs. C. told me. I sure hope her test results come out okay. She may get shipped out after pulling that little stunt. Man, that was stupid. And you too! Where's your head, girl?"

"No, I don't mean about Sooze. It's about me."

Morgan paused, her freckled face troubled. "*You're* not leaving, are you?"

"No, it's nothing like that. I did something last night that I had never done before. In fact, I thought I would *never* do it."

"Now what? Did you get yourself into more hot water?"

"No, nothing like that." Skye shook her head and took a deep breath. "Well, that truck accident made me think things through. All that stuff you and the Chambers have been telling me about God and all—well—all of a sudden, it sank in. I mean about needing God in my life, just like you said, and last night at the hospital I asked Jesus Christ to forgive me and to come into my life. I can't believe it, Morgan, but I feel like a whole new person. Like you've been telling me, it is *so* cool."

Nothing came out of Morgan's open mouth, and her eyes grew wide as she stared at Skye.

"You're kidding!" Morgan finally screeched. She dropped the cream tin and cloth in her lap and reached her arms toward Skye. "That is *so* great!"

"Ow!" Skye said as the two embraced. She pulled away sharply. "I am one big bruise."

"Sorry," Morgan said, "but that is such great news! Wait till Pastor Newman and the kids at church hear this. They've all been praying for you, you know. Even Chad."

"Chad?" Skye felt her face flush.

"Yeah, you heard me. The one and only Chad Dressler," Morgan giggled. "You know, he really likes you. I mean—he really, *really* likes you. Wait till he hears that you've become a Christian. He'll be totally impressed. And wait till he gets a look at the new you!"

"Very funny!" Skye replied. Then said softly. "I like him too, sort of."

"Sort of?" Morgan cackled as she picked up the saddle cream and cloth. "Sort of? Yeah, right. Every time his name is mentioned you turn five shades of red. I think you've got a crush on him. Anyway, I'm so glad you've become a Christian. Now you're my sister for real—my sister in Christ."

For once Skye was glad it rained in Shade Valley for the next three days. Watching Morgan ride would have been pure agony, but Skye's battered body wouldn't have even been able to sit on Champ. By the end of the week, the rain stopped. Feeling well enough to ride, Skye joined Morgan for a quick breakfast and headed to the barn. While low clouds hid the summer sun, they worked their horses in the large paddock, practicing for the upcoming horse show at the Snyder County Fair.

Morgan had just finished working Blaze in barrel racing and now sat on her mount, watching Skye practice for the Advanced Trail Class. Skye, in the center of the field, was engrossed in maneuvering Champ through a wooden gate between two posts.

"Careful, Skye," Morgan cautioned. "Champ tends to swing his rump too far to the left when you reach for the gate. If he bumps that post, you'll get docked some points!"

"Got it," Skye replied. "I'll try it again, this time a little slower." Skye positioned the horse carefully and reached down, gently swinging open the gate.

"Easy, Champ," she said. She rubbed his belly with her left leg; at the same time she tugged his reins to the right, prompting him to step sideways. Carefully, she nudged him through the narrow opening and turned him around. She reached down for the gate and clicked it closed while her horse stood like a statue.

"Voilà!" Morgan cheered. "That one was too perfect. Too bad you can't videotape it and send it to the judges. You'd take first place!"

Skye laughed as she jogged Champ toward Morgan. "He'll do it again," Skye insisted as she reached down and stroked the horse's silky mane. "This wasn't the first time. And he's been great with the water obstacle and the log step-over. I just need to catch up with his brilliance!"

"How's it going, girls?" a man's voice yelled from the backyard.

Skye turned to see Mr. Chambers walking toward them from the house. "Great, Mr. C.—uh, Dad," Skye yelled back. "Want to see Champ do the gate thing?"

"And Blaze is still blazing up a storm in her barrel cuts, Mr. C. You want to see a run of that too?" Morgan asked.

"I've got some work to do first," Mr. Chambers said, leaning up against the fence. "Maybe later in the afternoon when I get done."

"Did you bring Sooze home?" Skye asked.

"Yes, we did." Mr. Chambers' face grew deadly serious.

"Well, how is she? Does she get to stay here?" Morgan asked.

"Yeah," Skye added, "and *where* is she?"

"Skye, she wants to see you alone," Mr. C. said as he pointed toward the picnic grove next to the house. "She's over there. You go ahead, and I'll cool down Champ."

"What's the matter?" Skye asked as she dismounted. "Does she have to leave? Is she okay? What's going on?"

Morgan prodded Blaze and they started walking away. "I'll wait for you over at the barn, Mr. C."

Mr. Chambers crawled between the boards of the fence and took Champ's reins. "Sooze wants to tell you herself. Now go on," he gestured again, "she's waiting."

Beyond the fence, Skye could see the towering pines swaying around the picnic pavilion in the breeze. A lone figure, her back toward the field, stood by the pavilion.

"Sooze!" Skye tried to yell. She squeezed through the fence boards and pushed her body as fast as it would go across the lawn, over the bridge at the stream, and to the grove. By the time she got there, Skye was gasping for breath, her nostrils filled with the heavy, moist scent of pine.

I hope Sooze isn't in terrible trouble, she thought anxiously. *We never should've taken that truck!*

"Sooze!" Skye gasped a quick breath. "What's going on? Do you have to leave?"

chapter seven

S ooze turned slowly, her bruised face flooded with
tears. Her body, covered with black and blue scrapes
and bruises, looked just like Skye's.

"They did a whole bunch of tests." Sooze's voice sounded
strangled. "I've got a brain tumor—and I'm scared."

"A—what?" was all Skye could say. Disbelief threaded
its way through every inch of her aching body.

"A tumor. They found this thing in my head. That's
what's been giving me the terrible headaches."

Sooze sat down at the table, lowered her head onto
her arms, and began to sob. Still standing, Skye felt para-
lyzed by what she had just heard.

Sooze has a brain tumor? Skye's thoughts were racing,
groping for the right words to say—any words to say.

"Just be a friend in the tough times," Pastor Newman's
words from one of his sermons prodded Skye's memory.
"Jesus is your best friend, and he's always there. You too
can be that kind of friend to someone in need." Skye lowered herself gently and slipped an arm around Sooze.

As though God were weeping too, the skies opened
and raindrops pelted the carpet of pine around the

pavilion. With the rain, the air immediately grew cooler. Skye took a shaky deep breath. In seconds, a steady downpour brought distant thunder.

Sooze raised her head and wiped her eyes with her fists. "What am I going to do, Skye?"

Skye squeezed Sooze's shoulder. "I don't know," she answered. "But I do know someone who can show you what to do."

"Who?" Sooze's voice filled with hope. She turned and looked at Skye.

"God," Skye said.

Sooze's eyes, bloodshot and troubled, searched Skye's. "What?"

"I said God can help you."

Sooze slid away from Skye and gave her a nasty scowl. "Where are you coming from with this God stuff again? I told you the other day I didn't want to hear it! If God is so great, why would he let this happen to me?"

"I don't know—"

"Well—when you've got some answers, let me know," Sooze cried. "I'm the one with this thing growing in my head! I don't need anyone shoving religion down my throat along with everything else. Got it?"

"Got it," Skye said sadly. "But I want you to know that I'm here for you—and God is too."

Skye studied the brilliant blue sky that had come after the afternoon rain. She took in a lungful of cool evening air as she stood with Mrs. Chambers on the lopsided front porch of Sooze's mother's house.

"Well, aren't you a sight for sore eyes! Look at those bruises." Skye could hear Mrs. Bodmer, even over the television chatter inside the house.

"Thanks for caring!" Skye heard Sooze snapping back.

A few seconds passed before Sooze came back to the doorway and said, "Mom says it's okay to come in."

Skye followed Sooze and Mrs. Chambers into a living room stacked with boxes and newspapers. Mrs. Bodmer lay on a haggard brown sofa that looked like a prop from a haunted house. Her pudgy body, dressed in a cherry-red halter top and jean shorts, absorbed the breeze from a fan. Her frizzy hair swirled in the breeze, and her stubby, ring-clad fingers, now decorated with long purple fingernails, held a drink in one hand and a cigarette in the other.

"Come on in," Mrs. Bodmer's gruff voice ordered above the noisy TV, "and shut the door tight. We don't need any more flies in here!"

"It's good to see you again," Mrs. Chambers said loudly above the noisy TV. Sooze flopped into a sagging green chair and closed her eyes. Her head rested back on the dirty upholstery.

Mrs. Chambers continued, trying to be heard. "We need to talk to you about your daughter, Mrs. Bodmer! About her progress so far, and—well—her health!"

Mrs. Bodmer clicked off the TV, inhaled on her cigarette, and blew out a stream of smoke from her nose. Folding her arms, she squinted through the last puff of smoke that blew back in her face.

"Yeah, how's the kid doing? When I called the hospital this morning, they said she was sleeping, so I didn't want them to wake her. So what's going on?" She looked at Sooze with obvious suspicion. "You aren't getting into more trouble, are you, Susan? From the looks of you, trouble should've been your middle name!"

Heavy silence hung over the room.

"Skye, why don't you and Sooze find something to do, so Mrs. Bodmer and I can talk alone?"

"Sure," said Skye. Sooze reluctantly pulled herself out of the green chair, and the girls disappeared up the stairs to Sooze's old room.

Mrs. Chambers shifted from one foot to the other and then took a seat in the chair Sooze had vacated.

"Mrs. Bodmer, I have some troubling news. The doctors ran some tests on Susan while she was at the hospital."

"Tests?" Mrs. Bodmer said. She took a gulp from her can.

"Yes," Mrs. Chambers said. "We had a meeting with two different doctors earlier today, and they think Sooze has a brain tumor."

"A brain tumor?" Slowly, Mrs. Bodmer sat forward onto the edge of the sofa, set her can on the coffee table, and eyed Mrs. Chambers skeptically. "That's ridiculous!" she snorted. "What are you people trying to pull?"

"I assure you, it's true," Mrs. Chambers answered. "I know this is a shock."

"Now wait a minute. You're telling me my kid has a brain tumor? Does that mean an operation?" Mrs. Bodmer asked.

"No. Surgery isn't an option because of the location of the tumor. Next week the doctors want to run another series of tests, and if the results are the same, Sooze will need to begin chemotherapy and then radiation. The doctors would like you to come in with us at that time, so they can go over the test results with all of us."

"Well, how much is that going to cost me?" Mrs. Bodmer scowled. "I don't have any insurance, you know. And how do they know it's a brain tumor anyway? It could be a mistake."

"That's the reason for running a second series of tests," Mrs. Chambers said, "just to be sure. Mrs. Bodmer, I hope you realize that this is serious. Hopefully, with the treatments, she'll be okay. The tumor is what's been giving her the headaches. And the costs will be covered by the state since Sooze is in foster care."

Mrs. Bodmer stared at Mrs. Chambers. Then she returned to her original position on the sofa and took a long drink. "Susan isn't going to die, is she?"

"I hope not," Mrs. Chambers answered. "We're praying for her."

At the mention of prayer, Mrs. Bodmer sniffed loudly. "Great," she huffed sarcastically. "God's done so much for us in the past."

"Mrs. Bodmer," Mrs. Chambers continued, "the doctors are very hopeful that the treatments will curb the growth of the tumor. We're all hoping they have found it in time. Sooze knows about all of this. It's an awfully big deal for a kid her age. She really needs all the support we can give her right now."

Sooze and Skye reappeared on the stairs and slowly made their way back to where the women were sitting. Mrs. Bodmer stared intently at her daughter and then took one last puff on her cigarette before putting it out.

"Now wait!" She shook her head and drew her hands through her hair, flattening it against her head before it went back to its dance with the fan. "This is all going too fast." She studied Sooze again. "You mean my kid's so sick that she needs radiation and chemo?"

"Sooze, I've told your mother what's going on with you."

Mrs. Bodmer looked Sooze up and down one more time. "Susan, this isn't one of your dirty tricks again, is it?" Mrs. Bodmer growled. "If it is, it isn't one bit funny."

"I assure you it isn't," Mrs. Chambers said. "Sooze didn't cause this. It just happened."

"Don't worry, Mumsy," Sooze said sarcastically. "It's going to be loads of fun. First, I'll lose my hair, and then, I'll be throwing up my guts. Who knows—maybe I'll even die. That would be a lucky break for you, wouldn't it?"

Mrs. Bodmer reached for another cigarette and her lighter.

"Well, isn't life grand!" she hissed. "Like I don't got enough trouble. Now I got a sick kid."

"Before we leave," Mrs. Chambers said, "we'd like to pray with you and Sooze. Prayer always helps in times like these when we don't know which way to turn."

Mrs. Bodmer took another drink and then scowled.

"No thank you!" she harped. "I've never had a need for God, and I don't need him now. You can just take your prayers and be on your merry way. No god would let this stuff happen to me."

"I'm sorry you feel that way," Mrs. Chambers said. "God has helped me through some pretty tough times. He—"

"I said no!" Mrs. Bodmer shouted. "Like I said, you can just get on down the road!" Then she looked at Sooze. "And you let me know what's going on, okay?"

Sooze rolled her eyes and without as much as a glance at her mother headed out the front door, letting the screen door slam behind her. Without a word, Skye started toward the door.

Mrs. Chambers turned to leave, still looking at Mrs. Bodmer. "Let us know if you can go to the hospital with us next week. It would be good for you to hear the information directly from the doctors. And, of course, you're always welcome to come out to Keystone Stables for a visit. I'm sure Sooze would appreciate that."

Mrs. Bodmer turned on the TV with the remote control. Again sitcom laughter blasted through the room.

"Yeah, thanks," she slurred, settling into her couch. "Call me."

"We certainly will," Mrs. Chambers said.

chapter eight

Skye, look at this cool game I'm playing on the Internet." Morgan worked the computer keyboard like a pro. "It's called Asteroids."

The walls of the Chambers' game room vibrated with the noise of electronic laser blasts.

"Yeah, I've done that at the mall zillions of times." Skye called above the noise of her own Nintendo game. "One time I scored thirty thousand before I got zapped."

"I wonder how Sooze is," Morgan said.

"I don't think she feels too hot, especially since her first treatment. Man, did she throw up after that! And her poor hair. She looks like a scarecrow with a bad hair day."

"I hope the doctor has a good report. It's been two weeks since the chemo."

Skye glanced at the wall clock above the computer. "She and Mom ought to be back soon. We could all use some good news. I've never known anybody before who had a brain tumor. Kind of scary, isn't it?"

"Yeah. But I know God could help Sooze if she'd just let him. It has to be scary without having him on your team."

"Yikes! Get over there!" Morgan said to the screen.

The outside door to their right opened, the girls oblivious to it.

"Hey, what's happening?" Mrs. Chambers spoke above the game racket as she walked up behind Skye. "Hard at work helping Tom paint the fence, I see," she teased.

"Oh, we're going to help him in just a minute," Skye said, "as soon as these last games are done. Where's Sooze?"

"She'll be down in a minute," Mrs. Chambers answered. "She wanted to do something first. By the way, girls, I have sandwiches in the fridge down here if you want to eat before you attack the paint can."

Skye's game came to a crashing halt. She shut it down and followed Mrs. Chambers to the kitchenette.

"Mom, what did the doctor say about Sooze?"

Mrs. Chambers opened the refrigerator and pulled out a plate of sandwiches and a pitcher of iced tea. "Well, the doctor is quite hopeful that we caught this thing in time. He plans to give Sooze three more chemo treatments followed by radiation. That's supposed to shrink the tumor or kill it all together. They're pretty optimistic. I just wish Sooze's mother would join the process."

Morgan came in at the tail end of the discussion. "How often will she get those treatments?"

"Once a month," Mrs. Chambers answered, handing wet wipes to the girls. "That's all a body can handle."

"Yeah," Skye said, pulling paper plates from a cupboard, "but it doesn't seem to be working with Sooze. She threw up her guts, and her hair's falling out in gobs." Skye ran a hand through her hair, pulling a lock forward to study a few strands. "That would freak me out—I don't think I could handle that."

"Yeah, no hair would be awful," Morgan agreed.

"Girls, when your life's at stake, you look at things in a whole different light," Mrs. Chambers said. "Which would you choose? Your hair or your life? Getting sick

60

and losing your hair is part of the process, unfortunately. Sooze needs our prayers and support. Just encourage her as much as you can. She needs some good friends right now." She poured iced tea into three paper cups and smiled. "Let's pray over this feast, and we'll dig in."

Skye bowed her head and prayed. "Dear God, please help Sooze to feel better and get well, and thank you for this food. Bless it in Jesus' name. Amen."

"Hey, guys," Sooze's tired voice said.

Skye turned toward the doorway. Her gaze fell on Sooze, who had lost considerable weight, her skin was pallid, and her eyes seemed sunken more deeply into her thin face. But something was very different.

"Sooze," Skye exclaimed. "You have hair! Where— how—when?"

"Wow!" Morgan added. "That is too, too much! How did you get hair that fast? It's got to be a wig. Right?"

"Morgan, sometimes your brilliance knocks me out," Sooze slurred as she slowly squared a sky-blue cowboy hat on her wig. "They told me at the hospital that you guys wouldn't even notice the difference from my real hair."

"It's true," Mrs. Chambers said.

Skye took a gulp of tea. "It looks so much like the real thing, the kids at church won't even notice. Too cool!"

"Would you like a ham sandwich, Sooze?" Mrs. Chambers said.

"No, I'm not hungry," Sooze forced out, "just tired."

"Why don't you go lie down for a while," Mrs. Chambers suggested. "I'll wake you when we're ready to go to Maranatha. How does that sound?"

"I've got nothing better to do," Sooze complained. "Of course, I could go throw up for a while. Oh, sorry. I forgot you were eating."

"No problem." Skye went on eating her sandwich.

Mrs. C. smiled sympathetically. "Sooze, tell you what I'd like to do—that's if—and a big *if*—you feel better tomorrow. I've been thinking a lot about you and your horse situation. Maybe Stormy isn't the horse for you after all. I know the doctor wants you to take it real easy and not exert yourself. We'll be helping you with your chores. And as far as riding is concerned—"

Sooze's eyes looked like they were ready to jump out of her head. "Don't tell me I can't ride the horses!"

Skye swallowed quickly and said, "Sooze, take it easy, but Mom's right. Maybe she would let you ride if you started with a smaller horse that's trained in a completely different way. Pepsi might be just right for you, right Mom?"

"Yes. That sounds like a good solution." Mrs. Chambers smiled.

"She's a beautiful Blood Bay mare trained in Western only," Skye went on, "and she's a super trail horse with a lazy walk and easy gait. She'd never run off with you. Of course, you'd have to take it easy too. No horse enjoys a kick in the ribs. It's a wonder Stormy didn't buck you off a few weeks ago!"

"What does 'Blood Bay' mean?" Sooze asked.

"It means Pepsi is dark reddish-brown," Morgan said.

"Like a Pepsi Cola with a shot of cherry," Skye added. "The 'bay' part means that she has a black mane and tail. Oh, and guess what? Pepsi is Champ's mommy. Right, Mrs. C?"

"Right. They both come from a long line of champion Quarter Horses. And, like I was saying, if you feel better tomorrow, we'll start riding lessons again, this time with Pepsi and, hopefully, a new attitude. What do you say?"

Sooze smiled weakly. "Great," she managed to say, raising her thumbs slowly.

Mrs. Chambers cleared the counter. "Okay, that's what we'll do. By the way, if you decide you want to eat later, just help yourself. There's iced tea here too. Now why don't you try to get some rest?"

"Sounds like a plan." Sooze's eyes managed a hopeful twinkle. "See you guys later."

A few days later, on a beautiful August afternoon, Skye and Sooze rode their horses through the woods. Ahead of the girls, Tippy and Tyler ran wildly, making frequent stops to sniff every tree and rock they could find.

"Sooze, I think you'll do great in that Beginner's Showmanship Class at the horse show," Skye said, trying to be reassuring. "That thing in your head has slowed you down just enough to make you a greenhorn with an ounce or two of horse sense. After only a few weeks, you act like you've been hanging with horses all your life."

"I guess this brain tumor did do *one* good thing," Sooze said, tapping her hard hat. "No more kicking horses in the ribs. Now it takes all my energy just to crawl on and click my tongue to say go." She reached down and stroked the coarse black mane on Pepsi's nodding head. "I'm trying not to show it, but I'm kinda nervous over this horse show. You really think I can do it? What if I goof up? What if I'm even too tired to stand?"

"Just relax, will you? Remember, you won't even be riding Pepsi. All you have to do is lead her around the show corral, square her up, and then blend into the saw-dust. The judge will be looking at the horse, not you. Your most important part is getting her ready *before* the show. Brushing and oiling, polishing hooves, grooming her mane and tail. If you do a good job, Pepsi will be the star of the show. With a horse that's built like her, you could come home next week with a ribbon to match your Stetson. Besides, I'll help you."

The sound of squeaking saddles and clanking bridles accompanied the girls out from under a canopy of trees into a sun-drenched field. Skye loved the meadow with its wildflowers, tall grasses, and the scent of scrub pines. They rode toward a campsite nestled at the base of three rolling hills in the distance, while the dogs leaped in the grass like dolphins.

The girls dismounted at the campsite, near a chuck wagon resting in a cluster of pines. To the wagon's left, nestled against a hill, stood an outdoor chapel with rows of hewn-out logs for pews. In the center of the chapel, a stone cross stood tall on a pile of mountain stone.

The altar, Skye thought. *That's where I found out what real love is all about.*

"Wow! This place is awesome." Sooze exclaimed.

"This is Piney Hollow," Skye said. "The Chambers use it for picnics, church gatherings, and youth retreats."

"Youth retreats?"

"Yeah, kind of like camping or cookouts with the Youth for Truth club from church. Hey, I just remembered," Skye's voice bubbled with excitement. "There's going to be a retreat here in the fall with the church kids. It's Friday and Saturday. The girls sleep in the loft of the barn, and the boys do their macho thing out here in tents and sleeping bags. All the kids will be here—Morgan, Robin, Melissa, Doug, Chad." Skye's face flushed, thinking about Chad. "Remember? You met them all at church."

"Yeah." Sooze scanned the area like a lost child looking for her mother. "But what do you do out here for two days? Watch the grass grow?"

The girls tied their horses to a hitching post and hung their hard hats on the saddle horns. They walked around the campfire area before Skye answered.

"Well, all the chow, including breakfast, will be cooked over a fire right here. Have you ever had eggs and bacon fried like that?" Skye asked.

"My mom and I never exactly went camping."

"It's *so* great! Mom even makes biscuits over the campfire. After breakfast we usually go hiking and, of course, we have horses for trail riding. We spend a lot of time sitting around the campfire here and singing camp songs. Chad brought his guitar the last time, and Bobby brought his harmonica. Pastor Newman comes for supper on Friday. Then he talks to us at the chapel area." Skye plopped down on a stump and grabbed a stick to poke at a pile of ashes in the center of the fire circle. "Probably the first thing we'll do on Friday is go on a hayride."

Behind her, Sooze found a wooden crate and pulled it up next to Skye. "No way! You mean—that's it? Except for the horses, that sounds totally *boring*. Camp songs? Why can't we play our CDs and have some real fun?"

"Get off it, Sooze," Skye answered. She ran both hands through her hair. "The campouts are fun."

"Well, you never know. After all, I'll be there," she smiled devilishly. "In fact," she added while reaching into her jeans pocket and pulling out a handful of pills, "look what I have now."

"Where'd you get those?" Skye asked with alarm.

"What, you think they wouldn't give me something to kill the pain?" She took four tablets from her hand and popped them into her mouth. "Want some?"

"Sooze, you can overdose on that stuff. What are you trying to do—hurt yourself?"

"Hey, get off my back. Right now it's the *only* way I'm going to get through this. And you better not snitch."

"Like Mrs. C. isn't going to notice how fast they disappear."

"I'll just tell her my head felt like it was exploding. Man, I'm dying of thirst."

Skye rolled her eyes. "Yeah, it's a real scorcher today," she said in a feeble attempt to change the subject. "We should've brought canteens."

chapter nine

The excitement of the week-long Snyder County Fair ran through Skye's veins like electricity in a string of party lights—fun rides, pizza, and carnival games in perfect weather. But nothing made her heart pump as fast as the sights and smells of the horse show held every afternoon. For months, she and Champ had practiced for the Advanced Trail Class.

Skye's class finished and the gate opened, allowing her and the rest on the field to exit the show ring. With her glowing smile, she maneuvered Champ around the perimeter of the corral past dozens of horse trailers. The Chambers, Morgan and Blaze, and Sooze with Pepsi had all clustered along the show ring fence, waiting for Skye to join them.

Skye's hair, drawn back into a tight bun, rested securely under a suede cowboy hat, complete with hawk feather and leather braid. Her leather-fringed vest over a checkered shirt had the number "65" pinned on the back. Her blue necktie, cowhide gloves, and polished leather boots made Skye a perfect match for Champ.

Champ's shiny bridle with blue brow band set off a leather-cut saddle with a poncho roll highlighting his glistening sorrel coat. A lather of sweat added to Champ's sparkle as he tossed his head and snorted, showing off the shiny red ribbon attached to his cheek strap.

"Way to go, Skye!" Mr. Chambers applauded.

Mrs. Chambers patted Champ's neck. "In that tough class, second place is something to be proud of."

"Awesome," Sooze said, holding Pepsi's lead chain.

Morgan smiled underneath her tan Stetson, her folded arms resting across the horn of her saddle. "I told you the gate would be no big deal."

"Yeah, thanks, guys." Skye glanced at the packed grandstand and back. "The only problem we had was the water obstacle. Did you see Champ pause and then step to the side just a little? I think that cost us the blue ribbon."

"Nonetheless, you did a great job," Mr. Chambers said. "By this time—"

"Attention, ladies and gentlemen," the loudspeaker blared, "all contestants for the Beginner's Showmanship Class please line up at the east gate. Calling all contestants for the next event, the Beginner's Showmanship Class."

Skye glanced at the grandstand again, looking for Chad. When she didn't see him, she focused back on Sooze, whose pallid face portrayed a strange mixture of panic and courage.

Sandwiched between the horse and the fence, Sooze fussed with Pepsi's halter and arranged the horse's banded mane one last time. Sooze's blue Stetson sat squarely on top of her wig. A black necktie, red plaid shirt, jeans with a silver belt buckle, and black cowboy boots had totally changed her looks. Somehow, Sooze's painfully thin frame looked stunning. Pepsi's blood-bay coat shimmered, and her black tail had been groomed to silky perfection.

"How do you feel?" Skye asked Sooze.

"Like I'm going to throw up." Sooze made a face. "Not from the chemo. From my stomach doing back flips."

Mrs. Chambers walked to Pepsi and checked the halter buckle. "All I can say is thank the Lord your treatment was in the middle of last week. It gave your body time to recuperate. You do feel strong enough to do this, don't you?" Mrs. Chambers looked into Sooze's eyes.

"I'm going in there if I have to crawl," Sooze said nervously.

Morgan laughed, stroking Blaze on the neck. "Hey, maybe you can start a Beginner's Turtle Class!"

A preoccupied Sooze shifted her attention to the gate. "I think I ought to go. They're all lining up."

"Let's say a quick prayer," Mr. Chambers said when he finished checking the last of Pepsi's hooves.

While Mr. C. prayed, Skye watched Sooze with half-closed eyes. Her stare never wavered from the ring.

A little prayer would help you right about now! Skye thought.

"Amen," Mr. Chambers finished. He and his wife backed away from Pepsi. "Now take your time, Sooze, and listen carefully to the judge."

"Yeah," Skye injected, "this is no time to be doing your own thing. Be cool."

"I don't have enough energy to do my own thing, thank you," Sooze joked while leading the horse away. "Pepsi will do her own thing, and we'll be back with a blue ribbon. You'll see."

"Careful, and don't rush!" Mrs. Chambers called.

"And try to get in the center, right in front of the judge when you line up," Morgan yelled. "Let him get a real good look at one gorgeous hunk of horse flesh!"

Sooze led Pepsi toward the gate at the other end of the corral. The big, bold number "17" on Sooze's back distinguished her from the rest of the intermingling pack.

"Five — no, six others," Skye said, pointing. She tugged the reins and turned Champ toward the ring. "A piece of cake for Pepsi."

Mrs. Chambers leaned over the top rail of the fence. "It all depends on Sooze. Pepsi's got the confirmation to win this class hands down, but I'm not sure Sooze is thinking straight. Tom, did you get a good look at her eyes? She's been into her pain pills again. I should have locked them up. This morning I noticed they're disappearing faster than cotton candy," she said seriously.

"Yeah, I noticed too," Mr. Chambers agreed as he squared his Stetson. "This is no time to be taking a trip *without* your horse. I think she's going to learn a good lesson — but it breaks my heart."

"Look at her butting into the center of the pack." Morgan said. "I didn't mean for her to do it *that* way. I bet she never even said excuse me."

Skye sighed and shook her head in agreement as she studied the contestants leading their horses single file into the show ring.

Pintos, grays, blacks, and browns, each one prettier than the next, filed in, accompanied by contestants in a rainbow of Western attire. But no horse showed off its muscular perfection better than Keystone Stables' blue-ribbon mare. Unfortunately, Pepsi appeared to be led by a kid who staggered into the ring like her boots were stuck in mud.

"Something tells me this is *not* going to be fun to watch." Skye frowned deeply.

Intermingled with a barrage of whinnies and billows of dust, the seven entries paraded single file into the ring. They walked, jogged, backed their horses, and finally squared them up in the center of the corral. By this time, Sooze had lost the center position to others who cleverly maneuvered their horses in front of her as she struggled to circle the ring. Now she found herself next to last as the judge started his close inspection at the other end of the line. As she had been trained to do, Sooze tugged on Pepsi's lead chain, prompting the horse to stand at attention. But ignoring the next step in her training, Sooze failed to check Pepsi's four legs. The front two lined up perfectly. The back two legs stood in a half stretch, the left one far ahead of the right. The horse's stance and perfect confirmation were thrown completely off.

"Sooze, check her back legs!" Skye yelled.

"Don't bother," Mrs. Chambers said. "We're too far away. I don't think she'd listen if she were standing right by this post. Sooze is in her own little world."

"Maybe before the judge gets to that end, she'll wake up and check the legs," Mr. Chambers said hopefully.

Morgan's despair rivaled the others in their tightly knit group. "She's going to blow it."

Slowly the judge worked his way down the line, checking each horse's shape, eyeing it from the front, back, and sides, checking its teeth. In front of Pepsi, he raised his clipboard and pen just as Sooze yanked the lead chain. The sudden jerk sent Pepsi into a panic. She pranced in circles with Sooze frantically attempting to quiet her down. The judge stepped back in apparent frustration, and Skye could tell he was not at all amused.

"Uh, oh," Skye moaned. "Look at the judge's face."

Mr. Chambers raised his hat in frustration, scratched his head, and then squared his hat across his eyes. "Yep, she blew it all right. I know that judge, and he does not like to wait until you decide to square up your horse."

In minutes, the judge finished his tally. The loudspeaker announced the winners, the exit gate opened, and Sooze led Pepsi out and around the corral, returning empty-handed to the Chambers.

"That stupid judge!" Sooze yelled as she tied Pepsi to the fence. "He doesn't know good horseflesh when he sees it. He must be blind!"

Skye rolled her eyes. "Pepsi had every horse beaten without even blinking. *You* blew it—big time! You have to keep your horse still when the judge is standing right in front of you. Duh!"

"All right, you two," Mrs. Chambers interrupted. "It's over. No use crying over it. But Sooze, we hope you have learned something important today. If you don't have your head screwed on right, even the simplest of tasks can defeat you. I think you know what I mean, don't you?"

"I didn't do anything!" Sooze remarked. "It was all that stupid judge's fault!"

"Sooze, I think your day at the fair is over," Mrs. Chambers said sternly. "Tom and I are going to load the horses, and you'll be going home with me."

"Why?" Sooze questioned.

"You not only need to rest, but you also need to clear your head," Mrs. Chambers added. "But the first thing you need is some food in your system."

"I'm not hungry!"

"Sooze," her foster mother said more emphatically, "you need something in your stomach. Now, while Tom and I load the horses, I'd like you to go get something to eat. We'll give you a half hour. Then come back here, and you'll ride home with me."

Skye dismounted her horse and handed the reins to Mr. Chambers. "Thanks, Dad," she said. "I could use a burger or something. What do you say, Morgan?"

"Yeah, I could use something to eat too." Morgan glanced at the grandstand. "But I'm planning to meet some of the kids from church. They were sitting on the top row a while ago. They must be on their way over here now."

Mr. Chambers retrieved Morgan's wheelchair from the truck and set it on the dirt-packed walkway that led from the show ring to the rest of the fairgrounds. Morgan handed Blaze's reins to Mrs. Chambers while

Mr. Chambers loosened Morgan's legs from the Velcro safety strips on her saddle, gently slid her off into his arms, and placed her onto her chair.

"Thanks," Morgan said, glancing at Skye and Sooze. "Hey, you two, come with me. Skye and I don't have to be back in a half hour, do we, Mrs. C?"

"No, you have the rest of the afternoon," Mrs. Chambers said as she tied Blaze to the back of their hauling trailer. "Sooze is the only one who needs to go home."

"That's *so* not fair," Sooze whined.

"Duh. Life's not fair!" Skye said sarcastically. Then she asked casually, "Hey, Morgan, is Chad here?"

"He was supposed to be, but I haven't seen him yet," Morgan replied with a smile. "Come with me, and maybe he'll join us along the way."

Sooze crowded herself next to Skye. "No, we'll do our own thing. Thank you."

An artificial smile masked Skye's regret at not getting to see Chad. "Sooze and I can grab something to eat and then we'll meet you back here."

"Sounds good. Then we can do the fair thing with all the kids later, okay? Hey, here they come now." Morgan pointed across the field.

Sooze folded her arms angrily. "This stinks! You guys always get to have all the fun."

Mrs. Chambers walked from the back of the trailer like she was stomping ants. "Sooze, it's time you learned that there are consequences for unwise decisions and actions. That's the way it's going to be," she said emphatically.

"Come on," Skye said to Sooze, tugging her arm, "you only have a half hour. Don't waste it arguing."

Mr. Chambers pulled a wallet from his back pocket. "Do you girls have enough money?"

"I do," Morgan answered. She moved ahead slowly. "Where else can I spend that megabucks allowance you give me?"

"I've got money," said Sooze.

"Me too," Skye answered. "So I guess we're out of here."

Morgan stopped in front of Skye, her troubled eyes reaching beyond her smiling face. "Skye," she pleaded, "don't you think you should go with us?"

ell—" Skye hesitated. *I would like to see Chad,* she thought.

"Morgan, we don't need bodyguards," Sooze huffed. "Right, Skye?"

"Skye—" Mrs. Chambers' voice oozed with caution.

Mr. Chambers glanced back as he led Blaze to the trailer. "Remember, girls, you're on the honor system. We'll trust you as long as you don't give us any reason not to. And Sooze, you're already up to your neck in quicksand."

Morgan looked down the walkway. "Here come the guys now."

Sooze grabbed Skye's arm, abruptly pulling her away. "Come on. Let's go!"

"Later." Skye said to Morgan. *I'd rather be going with you,* she thought. She glanced back at the three approaching friends. Each yelled hello and waved.

"Come on!" Sooze tugged Skye's sleeve harder. "We're history."

"All right! All right!" Skye yanked free. "Give me a break. I'm coming. See you later!" she yelled warmly to the group.

The two girls soon blended into the bustling crowd, losing themselves among the buildings packed with antiques, arts and crafts, and farm gear. In the livestock section, pens and open barns overflowed with the commotion of prize calves, sheep, and pigs. Branching from the fair's core were narrow alleys blasting with music and hucksters yelling at passersby, "Win a prize every time!"

Food stands, squeezed into every plot, satisfied the whims of an endless parade of empty stomachs. Sour barn smells faded into those of barbecued chicken, pizza, and funnel cakes. Skye's mouth watered as she peered down every lane for a stand that sold burgers and fries.

"Over there!" Skye zeroed in on the Bill's Buffalo Burgers stand. "I love those, and they have great curly fries."

"I've got better things to do than eat," Sooze said, her dog-tired words sliding out from under her blue hat. "I've got a surprise for you."

"If it takes longer than twenty minutes, I'm not into it. Don't be any dumber than you've already been today. I'm getting a bison burger. What do you want?"

"Hey, I said I'm not hungry, and I mean it. Get what you want. Then we'll head over to the midway."

"Why? What's over there?" Skye asked as they walked toward the stand.

"Just wait and see." A silly smile flashed across Sooze's face.

"Don't tell me you want to get on some rides! You already get sick to your stomach from the chemo. Besides, we don't have enough time."

"Just hurry up."

Skye ordered a burger, fries, and chocolate shake. While they headed for the midway, Sooze carried the box holding the fries and shake. Skye scarfed down her food and gulped her creamy shake.

"This is too good." Her milky mustache confirmed her pleasure. "Want some?"

"Nope," Sooze said, balancing the cardboard tray while they weaved past a string of sideshows toward the Ferris wheel.

"Not that thing!" Skye griped through the last mouthful of food. She tossed the garbage in a trash can, and then her eyes followed rotating buckets on the humongous light-flickering wheel. "I can't believe you want—" Skye glanced at her watch. "Sooze, we only have ten minutes to get back! I don't even have time to see the motorbikes!"

"Just cool it!" Sooze demanded. She took the lead on a walkway behind the wheel. "Come on down here behind the restrooms."

"What are you doing?"

"I see them. They're here!"

"Who?"

"Come on. You'll see."

Skye trailed after Sooze, who puffed her way past the cinder-block bathroom building to a cluster of shady maples.

"Sooze!" *I am getting bad vibes*, Skye thought. Her panic now had nothing to do with the time.

"Hey, Sooze! Skye!" a voice bubbled from the shade of the trees. "Look at you two. Ride 'em cowboy! Where'd you get those rags?"

"Kenny, my man!" Sooze yelled, forcing her tired body toward the voice.

Skye squinted from the shade of her hat. She strained to focus on a couple of teenagers, one she didn't know. Beside the stranger stood a lanky boy who wore a green baseball cap flipped backward, a black T-shirt, and baggy jeans.

Kenny Hartzell! Skye remembered him all too well. *What's he doing here?*

As Sooze approached Kenny, his tattooed arms stretched to greet her with a high-five. Skye stepped forward and offered her own palms reluctantly.

"Hey, what's happening?" Sooze asked.

"This is awesome seeing you guys again," Kenny said.

"You better believe it," Sooze said, her thumbs already up. She looked behind her as if she were hiding something.

Skye squared her hat smartly over her eyebrows and stared at Kenny. "How did you get out of Chesterfield? Weren't you supposed to be there for eighteen months?"

"Hey, I know how to buck the system." Kenny pointed to himself with his thumb. "I walked the line, and they let me out early. Simple as pie." His braces displayed a deceptive smile, and then he looked to the girl standing to his left.

"This is Tanya Bell," Kenny said. "She's from Philly."

Skye studied the girl who stood half a head taller than Kenny. Her smooth face boasted two rows of perfect teeth and dimples that exploded when she smiled. A red-and-white tank top and jean shorts hugged her shapely body, and her gazelle legs stood posed in high-heeled sandals. She easily could have passed for a model. She cradled an orange and white teddy bear at least half her size in one arm.

"Hey, what's up?" Sooze said to the girl.

"Tanya? Cool," Skye said. "What brings you to Snyder County? I mean, this is horse country—a long way from the big city. The closest we get to excitement is watching the sun go down."

"This is my sixth summer at the fair," Tanya said. "When I was younger, I visited some cousins who lived near here. I don't know," she said resting her free hand on her hip, "I just like it here. Things slow down just enough to let me think. I met Kenny last summer, and we've been friends ever since."

"Yeah," Kenny added, "real good friends. She stays with some people that live a few doors down from us.

"Awesome," Sooze said.

"Yeah," Skye said, looking at her watch. "Sooze, we've gotta go *now*."

"What's up?" Kenny asked. "Hey, that's right! You two are foster kids now. And you're hanging out at the same house. Does 'mommy' want you home?" he teased.

"You guys aren't serious," Tanya laughed. "You actually have rules that you have to follow?"

"They aren't that bad," Skye said.

Sooze interrupted. "Kenny, did you know I have a brain tumor?"

"You're joking. For real?" he answered.

"Yeah, I've had chemo and everything," Sooze started to explain. "This is a wig I'm—"

"Do you two want a smoke?" Kenny interrupted.

"Sure," Sooze said. "I'm dying for one. It's been *forever*."

"Skye?" he asked.

"Ah—" Skye folded her arms.

Sooze rammed Skye with her elbow. "What's the matter with you? Our prison wardens aren't anywhere around. Go on. Relax and enjoy yourself."

"Nah," Skye said. "I don't even miss it."

"Maybe you farmers don't know how to have a good time!" Tanya laughed.

"Come on," Sooze said sharply to Skye. "Just like old times."

Kenny stepped backward, pulling out a bulging, gray backpack from behind a large tree. "I got something we can all enjoy in this heat." He opened the flap, pulled out a can of beer, and handed it to Tanya.

"Sooze," he said, pulling out another and tossing it to her.

She popped the seal and took a long guzzle.

"Skye," he said, flipping another can into her unsuspecting arms.

Skye juggled it, barely saving it from landing on the ground.

"C'mon girl!" Tanya taunted.

Skye reluctantly popped the tab and took a mouthful. As soon as Skye swallowed, her whole body cringed with a feeling she couldn't explain. Her mind brought her a wave of strange, new guilt.

"After you accept Christ, God is with you all the time," Dad Chambers had said in devotions a few weeks ago. "He is there to help you make the right choices. When you sin, you grieve the Lord, and you'll feel terrible."

Skye's stomach recoiled as if she had been kicked by a horse, and she stiffened in shame. A Bible verse from Pastor Newman's last sermon swept through her mind, haunting her with a new realization: *Therefore, if anyone is in Christ, he is a new creation; the old has gone, the new has come!*

She was no longer the same person she had been before becoming a Christian. A wave of nausea swept over her, and her eyes searched desperately for a garbage can to throw away the beer.

This is so not fun, Skye thought, her stomach churning. "Hey, you guys—"

"Skye Nicholson!"

Like a carefully aimed bullet, the voice shot through the air, down the walkway, and hit Skye right in the middle of her unsuspecting back. Suddenly, she felt sick for two reasons. It was a familiar voice. A very familiar voice.

chapter eleven

S ooze wasn't the only one to be grounded. Back home, Mrs. Chambers' blue eyes flashed during their emergency family conference.

"It's very interesting what the Lord allowed me to see," Mrs. C. said. "I walked out of the administration office after finishing some horse business and—bam!—there you two were under the trees. I certainly wasn't spying on you. I just happened to be at the right place at the right time."

Skye thought she'd die from the punishment of not seeing Champ for two weeks. She loved riding him, especially during the summer months. Worse than that, she had other feelings to deal with. She felt dirty inside; she had disappointed God. For days, she moped around the house while Sooze made light of their predicament and schemed her next move. Not until Skye, in the privacy of her bedroom, asked God to forgive her did she even come close to feeling right again. This being-a-Christian thing was serious business, and she had found out the hard way.

September came and with it Skye's freedom, and the excitement of a new year at Madison Middle School.

She also found herself more excited about spiritual things, soaking up Pastor Newman's sermons and Mr. Chambers' devotions. She read her own Bible and prayed every morning before facing the day and had a new determination to live for the Lord. She was also growing in her confidence to face any challenge because she and God were going to school arm in arm.

Skye saw Sooze very little during the day, not only because they shared no classes, but also because Skye had new interests. The old temptations were still there, but now she was making new friends, especially in the youth group, and she had even decided to join a few clubs. At home, Skye did spend time with Sooze, mostly to help her with her homework and to support her through her declining health and medical treatments.

October in Pennsylvania brought crystal blue skies and rolling hills blanketed with palettes of brilliant colors. With the fall youth retreat only a day away, Skye and Sooze rode their horses to Piney Hollow after school to help Mr. Chambers clean up. He was busy cutting the weeds around the campsite when Skye and Sooze rode up to join him.

"Hi, girls," Mr. Chambers said, turning off the mower and wiping his forehead. "What a beautiful day to work outside. This nice breeze is just right to cool off a hot cowboy. Thanks for volunteering to help me get this place in shape."

"Did we have a choice?" Skye giggled. She patted Champ and looked around at the blazing fall colors. "Just kidding."

"I'm too tired," Sooze said.

"And I don't think she's kidding," Skye added.

Mr. Chambers bent down and checked the gas level of the lawn mower. "Sooze, I know you have very little energy because of your treatments. I don't expect you to do much here. Just hand Skye the things she needs while she scrubs out the chuck wagon. You can give her moral support. Tie Champ and Pepsi in the shade over there. We have a lot of work to do."

The girls maneuvered their horses to a hitching post under the large scrub pines.

"Man, I hate to clean," Skye said to Sooze, "but this kind of cleaning isn't bad, out in the open and around the horses. Why don't you just sit and watch and keep me company. I can tell you're feeling pretty bad."

Skye dismounted and tied Champ to the railing. Leaning against the post, she slipped off her hard hat. Sooze slipped off hers as well. From a saddlebag, she pulled a red baseball cap to cover her bald head. She moved like she had cement in her boots, and even the simple task of securing Pepsi's reins was a struggle. Her body was bloated from the steroids that were meant to build up her strength.

"I only threw up once this morning," she said with a heavy breath. "It's been almost a week since my last chemo."

Skye balanced her hat on the saddle's horn and tied her hair into a ponytail. "You sure don't look like yourself. But I guess the steroids do help give you a little energy, don't they?"

"Yeah, about two ounces worth—one for each little finger," Sooze tried to joke.

"Well, I guess even that little bit helps."

Skye walked to the truck bed, where she filled two buckets with hot water from a large container. She poured Lysol into one bucket and grabbed a fistful of rags. Sooze had followed her over to the truck, but one look into her foster sister's eyes gave Skye a start. Sooze looked so tired.

"Here, you carry these and the broom." Skye yanked the rags from her pocket, handed them to Sooze, and picked up both buckets of water. "Victory over spiders!" she declared as she turned toward the chuck wagon.

While Mr. Chambers groomed the campsite, Skye swept out the wagon and scrubbed its insides. Sooze rested on a crate outside, handing Skye rags as she needed them. After retrieving fresh water and a batch of clean cloths, the girls sat inside the covered wagon. Sooze handed Skye cooking utensils and plastic containers one at a time while Skye scrubbed them clean. The late afternoon sun warmed the wagon, giving it a pale yellow tint.

Sooze smiled impishly, thinking ahead to her next words. "This place is so awesome. Speaking of awesome," she slipped in casually, "I'm meeting Jason Stine third period tomorrow."

"Jason Stine?" Skye's face clouded in disgust. "I was sure you'd put trouble behind you."

Sooze handed Skye a large metal ladle. "Well, our buddy Kenny got himself busted again. This time when they locked him up in Chesterfield, they probably threw away the key. I needed a new contact, so Jason was more than willing. Do you want to meet me fifth period in the gym bathroom?"

"Of course not," Skye said as she scrubbed the spoon in one bucket and then rinsed it in the second. She pulled it out and jabbed it in Sooze's direction with a very determined look. "I don't get why you're so set on making things worse for yourself."

Sooze grabbed the spoon and smothered it with a soggy towel. "What's it going to do, kill me? I figure the tumor's going to do that first. So what if I use a little something to get me through this?"

"You have plenty to help you get through this, Sooze," Skye responded. "You have me, Morgan, the Chambers, Pepsi, and God—if you would just give him a chance to show you that he can help."

"Skye, you're so *different* since you've been living here. I don't even know you anymore. They've really gotten to you, haven't they?"

"I told you before, Sooze, nobody *got* to me." Skye grabbed a bunch of utensils, plopped them in the soapy bucket, and started washing. "I've just learned so much about myself and God, and, well, I needed him on my side. When I accepted Christ after our accident—we could have been killed, you know—it just changed the way I look at things. I don't need *stuff* to make me feel good anymore. God is always there when I need him. He's the best friend I've ever had."

One at a time, Skye handed over the utensils. Sooze dried and placed them on the counter behind her.

"You know we've been learning about avoiding danger in youth group. Remember what Pastor Newman said? You can make bad choices and mess up your body."

"Nah, I don't remember anything from youth group. I'm usually in La-La Land. That church stuff isn't for me."

Skye whacked the bucket with a metal spoon in frustration. She wondered if she would ever be able to get through to her friend.

"Skye—" Sooze started to say.

Skye busied herself scrubbing an old tin coffee pot.

There was a long silence, which forced Skye to look up. "What?"

Out from the shadow of the ball cap, Sooze's face was covered in a steady stream of tears.

"What's wrong?" Skye slowly pulled the pot from the rinse bucket and wrapped it in a cloth.

"Do you ever think about dying?" Sooze cried.

"Sure. Sometimes. Doesn't everyone?"

"No, I mean really dying—like now." Sooze dried her eyes with an already drenched towel. "The doctors keep telling me that I'm okay, but I've got a bad feeling about this. I don't think I'm going to make it, and I don't know what's out there."

For once, Skye was speechless.

"I feel so alone," Sooze added.

"You have your mom . . . and all of us!" Skye spoke with more hope than she was feeling.

"How many times has *Mom* come to see me since I've been here?" Sooze's voice rose in anger. "How many times has she even called?"

Skye glanced upward, knowing the answer.

"That's right," Sooze said. "Zero! Nada! Zilch! She doesn't care. She never did."

"But you have us," Skye said. "And Pastor Newman and the people at church care. Everyone is praying for you."

"That doesn't help much when I'm lying in bed at night thinking about . . . do you really think there's a heaven?"

"Yes," Skye said strongly. "The Bible says there is."

"Then you don't just die," Sooze sniffled. "I mean, you go somewhere, don't you?"

"Yes. Everyone who accepts Christ goes to be with him. It couldn't be simpler. And it's wonderful there. No more crying. No more pain. Sooze, why don't you give your heart to God? Then you wouldn't have to worry about dying because you'd know you'd go to heaven."

"I've never thought much about it," Sooze said softly. "You heard my mom when we went to see her. She has no time for God. She always said we could make it on our own. I don't think she even believes he exists. I think part of her problem is that we know some people who say they're religious and all, but they have this long list of rules they try not to break. They live like they're in prison all the time."

"I'll tell you one thing, Sooze. I never thought about him much either before I came here. All I thought about was living it up, but I was so messed up from all the rotten things I had done. The truth is that I was having a lousy time instead of a good time. This God stuff all makes perfect sense to me now. I know that when I die, I'll go to be with Jesus. That is so cool. Why don't you give him a chance?"

"I'll think about it," Sooze said quietly.

"Hey, girls," Mr. Chambers said, popping his head into the back of the wagon. He glanced at his watch and then took in what the two girls had accomplished. "Wow! It looks and smells great in here. We've finally got a decent campsite. Why, I think I could eat off this floor. Great job, ladies! Let's pack up and head back for supper."

chapter twelve

eth, over here!" Skye said as she stood near one corner of the barn loft. Around Skye, the youth group girls chattered like birds, claiming their cherished spots to spend the night. The bed of hay quickly vanished under a sea of sleeping bags, backpacks, and MP3 players. The air pulsated with jokes, the latest school news, and the excitement of roughing it at Keystone Stables.

"Girls!" Mr. Chambers called from the bottom of the stairs. "Hay Wagon Number One leaving the station in five minutes."

"Hey, Melissa!" Skye yelled at a tall blonde, tiptoeing across the sleeping bags toward the steps. "Come here."

"What's up?" Melissa walked over to Skye, who met her halfway.

"Is Chad here? I didn't see him get off the bus."

"Yeah, he's here. He was in the back, protecting his guitar from the wild beasts." Melissa flashed her pretty smile and studied Skye from head to toe. "Although—the way you look, he'll have a hard time keeping his eyes on his guitar. Your dark hair looks terrific with that red sweatshirt. And where'd you get those boots?"

87

"At the mall." Skye ran her fingers through her silky hair, letting it fall casually onto her shoulders. "I always thought I looked okay in red."

"Okay is not the word," Melissa said. "More like awesome! Chad will be totally impressed."

The girls giggled their way into the flow of those who were already starting down the stairs. At the bottom, they joined one of the chaperones, Mr. Salem, and the boys who were meandering to each stall, looking at the horses, reaching cautiously to pet their noses. Skye made a beeline toward Champ, bubbling about how great a horse he was.

"Okay, kids!" Mr. Chambers shouted from the open doorway. "Wagon departing!"

The kids charged toward the door. Mr. Chambers barely managed to get out of the way before they rushed through the opening and jumped onto an open wagon fluffed with a soft bed of hay. Against the back railings, Morgan and Sooze already sat like two hens on a nest of eggs. The last ones to board were the chaperone and Skye, who found herself sitting near Chad. As usual when he was around, her face turned red hot.

Chad's brown eyes sparkled. "Hey, Skye!" he said.

"Hey," she said back. "Where's your guitar?"

"On the driver's seat with Mr. Chambers," he answered. His chipmunk smile and blond eyelashes seemed to light up the wagon. "I didn't want it smashed in the hay fight that I predict will happen with this bunch. So, how's it going?"

"Good. It's going good," she answered.

For the next hour, the wagon drawn by two work-horses from a neighboring farm meandered on dirt roads around and through the Keystone Stables property. On the hill behind the barn, the passengers enjoyed the beauty of autumn in Shade Valley that stretched for miles around them. The wagon passed the picnic grove, the pond, and crept through the red and orange canopy toward Piney Hollow.

Bouncing with every rut and bump in the road, the group laughed, sang songs, shared stories from school, and talked about football and soccer. Despite the excitement of it all, Skye found herself preoccupied with thoughts of Chad as she stared awkwardly at her boots, not knowing what to say to him.

Deep in thought, Skye hardly noticed the hay fight that had erupted until a wad of it hit her right in the face. She gasped and sputtered like a motorbike out of gas, spitting out hay dust. Then all in one motion she scooped up a handful of hay and pitched it toward the first target in her line of fire — Chad. Her reward was a handful of itchy hay dust down her sweaty back.

The wagon bounced along the trail with squeals of laughter and a dustbowl of flying hay. When it rounded the corner through the woods and pulled into Piney Hollow, Mrs. Chambers and Mrs. Salem were placing heaps of food on a large table in front of the chuck wagon. With the smell of hot dogs, baked potatoes, and roasted corn in the crisp fall air, the hay fight ended as fast as it had started.

The kids jumped off the wagon, dusted each other off, and gathered in a circle as Mr. Salem led them in prayer. Shoving each other in line, they filled their plates with the best that Piney Hollow's chuck wagon could offer and sat on sawed-off stumps around the campfire.

Skye, Melissa, Sooze, and Morgan sat in a cluster eyeing Chad and Bobby, who were engaged in a corn-eating contest. By the time supper came to an end, Pastor Newman pulled up in an RV. After a quick cup of coffee, he presented a short message to the group at the chapel. A question-and-answer period about the book of Jonah followed. Then the group was dismissed for some time to socialize.

Chad and Skye made their way back to the campfire. Chad poked at a cluster of coals in the fading flames.

"Pastor Newman sure knows his stuff. I always wondered why Jonah was so mad at God for sending him to Nineveh," he said. "I guess those Ninevites weren't exactly your friendly next-door neighbors. They would've chopped your head off pretty quick."

Skye grabbed a stick and stuck a marshmallow on the end. "Yeah, it does make more sense now. I always thought that story was a fairy tale. But a big fish really *did* swallow Jonah. Can you imagine being in a fish's stomach? Gross!"

They were both laughing when Sooze approached and sat down next to Skye.

"Hi, Sooze," Skye said with more enthusiasm than she actually felt. *This is so not the time to be crashing the party, Sooze!* she thought ungratefully.

Chad looked over past Skye. "Hey, Sooze, how are you doing?"

"So-so," Sooze forced out.

Skye smiled weakly.

Sooze smiled back. "Skye, I need to talk to you."

Skye ignored her and turned to Chad. "Bobby told me you just got hired at Jacob's Hardware Store."

Chad smiled. "Yeah, I'm saving for a car."

"Skye," Sooze said softly.

Skye turned toward Sooze and gave her a can-this-possibly-wait look. "What?!"

"I *really* need to talk to you—now."

Without wanting to, Skye noticed Sooze's posture—slumped over, the brim of her Stetson pulled down, tears dropping on her shirt.

"Excuse me, Chad." Skye was already turning toward Sooze.

"No problem," Chad threw his stick in the fire and stood. "I'll go see what the guys are doing."

"Okay, everybody!" Mr. Chambers announced right behind Skye. "Time for the scavenger hunt! Meet me over by the hitching post under the pines."

"Scavenger hunt?" Chad responded. "It's almost dark!"

Mr. Chambers' mustache twitched playfully. "I know, my good man. That's what makes it so much fun. Trying to find an acorn with the sun sinking fast is very tricky. But at least the bears don't usually come out until after dark."

"Bears?" Chad's smile melted into mock fear.

"Ah, he's just kidding," someone called out. But the tone didn't sound reassuring.

"I sure hope so!" Chad's glance swept the scene. "Whatever, I'm ready. Let's go — and in the opposite direction of the bears!"

"Are you two coming?" Mr. Chambers asked.

"In a sec," Skye said. "We have to do something first."

"Fine," Mr. Chambers said with an understanding smile. He joined Chad and walked to where the others were gathering.

Skye knelt beside Sooze. "What is it?" Skye whispered.

"I need to talk to you," Sooze's voice quivered. "Alone."

"How about over there?" Skye pointed toward the chapel. "There's nobody around."

The girls walked to the bench in front of the cross. Sooze sat in obvious pain, gasping for breath. Then she started to weep out loud.

Skye sat down next to Sooze and slipped an arm around her. "Did somebody say something?"

"It's nothing like that," Sooze said, wiping her nose on her sleeve. She glanced toward the cross. "All that stuff about God you've told me since I moved in here — it finally sank in tonight when I listened to Pastor Newman. I mean it really sank in. I want to invite Jesus Christ into my life, and I'm not just saying that 'cause I'm scared. I see now that I've been fighting against myself."

"Sooze, God loves kids like us. That's what's so neat about him. Jesus died so we could be at peace here on Earth and live with him forever someday in heaven."

Sooze studied the cross. "Well, what do I have to do? I've never belonged to a church. Do I have to join? I've never even prayed. How do I pray?"

"Just do what I did. It's not that hard, Sooze. Ask God right now to forgive you and wash away your sins. Jesus already took your punishment, so there's nothing for you to do but thank him for it and accept it. Just talk to him honestly. That's all he wants."

Unaware of the yells and laughter from the woods, the two friends talked and prayed. A sliver of pink from the setting sun shone through the trees, illuminating the cross as the two bowed their heads. For the first time in her life, Sooze prayed out loud. Opening her heart wide before God, she asked him to forgive her and to come into her life.

"Amen." Sooze said with a relieved tone in her voice.

"Sooze," Skye said, looking into her friend's eyes, "God just made you brand new on the inside. You'll never be the same again. You'll see."

The friends threw their arms around each other and cried tears of joy.

chapter thirteen

"We're going to a football game," Mrs. Chambers shouted above the noise and laughter of the TV in the Bodmer living room. "Sooze asked if we could stop by for a few minutes to see you."

Skye and Sooze plopped down on the floor and let Mrs. Chambers have the green chair. With November's chill and the threat of snow, all three were bundled up in heavy coats, on their way to Madison's last game.

Mrs. Bodmer had already nestled into her favorite spot on the sofa hours earlier. Her frizzy hair was now red. Purple fingernails held a cigarette that she puffed every few seconds.

Sooze's mother lifted the remote control and forced herself to click off the TV off. "I was wondering what brought you this way. I hope this isn't anything more than a social call." Her eyes shifted to Sooze. "And aren't you a pretty sight? What have you been eating to get so big so fast? You'll soon be as big as me, and that's saying something!"

"It's not from food, Mom," Sooze said. "It's from my meds."

"What meds?" she asked flippantly.

"Steroids," Skye said. "They help her fight the pain from the tumor."

Mrs. Chambers shifted her weight. "Sooze's medicines do strange things to her body, Mrs. Bodmer. But we didn't come to talk about that. Sooze wants to tell you something."

"What trouble are you in now?" Mrs. Bodmer snarled.

"I'm not in any trouble at all," Sooze replied calmly.

"This time Sooze has *good* news to tell you, if you can believe it!" Skye could not keep the delight from her voice.

Mrs. Chambers added, "She's been making some very good choices lately, and I think she should tell you about them herself. Go on, Sooze."

Mrs. Bodmer crossed her arms. "Well, what is it?" She stared glumly at her daughter.

Sooze leaned forward slowly and rested her elbows on her knees. "I've been learning all kinds of stuff at the Chambers' house, Mom, to help me get my head together. They've been telling me about God, and a few weeks ago, I asked Jesus Christ to come into my life."

"And what does that mean?" Mrs. Bodmer barked, running her free hand through her frizz. "Don't tell me you got religion now! That's all I need to hear!"

"It's not religion, Mrs. Bodmer," Mrs. Chambers said. "It's a personal relationship with God—the creator of the universe. When someone accepts what Christ did for us on the cross as Sooze did, God makes that person new, inside and out. Sooze is a different person now."

"Yeah," Skye added. "I accepted Christ too, and I've only been in trouble once since then. God gives—"

"Hey!" Mrs. Bodmer snapped. "I told you the last time that I didn't want to hear any of this God junk. My kid still have that tumor in her head? Huh? Look how much good God's doing her! Now if that's all you came to talk about, there's the door!"

"But, Mom," Sooze pleaded, "you don't understand. This is different. If you'd just listen—"

"That's it! No more. You got no business coming into *my* house and cramming this religion stuff down my throat." Mrs. Bodmer blew a short blast of smoke out her nose and scowled at Sooze. "And I'm surprised at you for falling for this baloney, Susan. What's the matter with you?"

"Mom," Sooze's voice cracked, "God is real—and he loves you!"

"Easy, Sooze," Mrs. Chambers warned.

"Yeah, and pigs can fly!" Mrs. Bodmer's face turned beat red. "If that's all you came to tell me, I'm not interested. Let me repeat it, so it's nice and clear. I'm not interested—period!"

"I'm sorry to hear that." Mrs. Chambers stood and zipped her coat. "All right, girls, I think it's time to go. But, Mrs. Bodmer, would you consider doing one thing for Sooze?"

"What?" Mrs. Bodmer said gruffly.

"Thanksgiving is in a few weeks. Would you come to our place for dinner? We'll have turkey and all the trimmings. If you like football, Tom will have games on all afternoon."

"Yeah," Skye agreed. "We'd love to have you. Wouldn't we, Sooze?"

"Please, Mom. I could show you my bedroom and the barn and the horse I ride."

"We'll even come to pick you up," Mrs. Chambers added.

"I'm busy!" Mrs. Bodmer fired back.

"We were never busy before on Thanksgiving," Sooze said. "We always ate frozen dinners and watched TV. What's different this year?"

"I told you I'm busy. Thanks, but no thanks." Mrs. Bodmer turned on the TV.

"Then how about Christmas?" Mrs. Chambers said loudly.

"I'm busy!" Mrs. Bodmer said even louder without thinking twice. "I'm just busy!"

Skye and Sooze followed Mrs. Chambers into the back of the Booster Club stand at the football stadium. In a red apron, Mr. Chambers stood at the stoves and labored over French fries in troughs of hot grease. Morgan sat in a corner peeling potatoes. Two adults at the front counter were selling fries like they were made of gold.

"Hey, it's about time you got here to help." Mr. Chambers smiled when he saw his wife. "I'm just about fried out. I'd give a month's salary for a hot dog right about now."

"You poor man," his wife kidded, "how you suffer for such a just cause as new band uniforms. Give me your apron, and you can go round up a hot dog. How about making that two?"

"Make it three!" Morgan laughed.

Mr. Chambers took off his apron and handed it to his wife before turning toward Sooze and Skye. "Girls, do you want a hot dog too? I might as well make it a half dozen."

The girls traded mischievous glances. "Nah," Skye said. "We're wondering if we could go get something to eat on our own. We'd like to hike around the field for a while. Maybe we'll see some kids from Youth for Truth. That's really what football games are for. Right?"

Mr. and Mrs. Chambers laughed, and Mr. Chambers walked toward the door.

"Well, in my day," he said, "let's see, that was about a hundred years ago, we went to football games to watch

96

the players make fools of themselves chasing that pigskin all around the field. I guess times have changed, haven't they, dear?"

Mrs. Chambers took off her coat, slipped the apron over her head, and tied it behind her back. She smiled affectionately at her husband. "You just don't know us girls, Tom. We go to games for things other than sitting and watching what happens to some dumb football on a field. Right, girls?"

"Right!" Skye answered.

"Right!" Sooze agreed.

Morgan pointed at the stove. "I'd rather peel potatoes next to these warm fryers any day than go out there and turn into an ice cube. Sitting in those cold bleachers just doesn't appeal to a lightweight like me. Don't forget my hot dog, Mr. C.—and that's with everything."

Tom Chambers grabbed his coat off a hook on the wall. "Three hot dogs with the works, coming right up!"

Skye gave Sooze a sheepish grin. "We'll just walk around and see if anybody from youth group is here."

"Oh, they're here," Morgan said. "They were hanging around just a few minutes ago. All except Chad. He's working tonight."

Too bad, Skye thought, but she hid her disappointment.

"Well, we'll look for the other kids if Sooze feels all right," Skye said it as if she didn't have a clue who Chad was.

"Yeah, no problem as long as we turtle walk," Sooze said, embarrassment peeking through each word. "I know I can make it around the field at least once."

Mr. Chambers dashed toward the hot dog stand, and the two girls headed off in the opposite direction. Skye took short steps to match Sooze's snail pace. They weaved around scrambling children and adults who carried cartons overflowing with food. After only half a lap, Sooze huffed like she had just run the last touchdown.

They stopped near one of the goal posts "to watch the game," or so Skye said.

"Hey, Sooze! Can you believe it? Madison is winning, fourteen to zip! I thought they were supposed to lose tonight." A sharp gust of frigid air swept through the stadium, forcing Skye's hands into her jean pockets.

Skye glanced at Sooze, who was pulling her baseball cap down tighter over her wig and shoving her hands into her own deep pockets.

Large fluffy snowflakes began to tumble from the pitch-black sky. Dancing to Madison's band, they swirled and bounced in front of the brilliant lights, dropping a curtain of white that easily distracted Skye's attention from what was happening on the field.

"Hey, it's snowing!" Skye could hardly contain her excitement.

"This is too awesome!" Sooze said, joy overshadowing her pain. "I love when it snows. Hey, ever go snowboarding?"

"No, but I've gone sledding a zillion times." In the same breath, Skye's next question cut to the heart of her deepest thoughts. "Sooze, ever think you could live with your mom again?"

"I don't know," Sooze's thoughts were far away. "I used to hate her, but I don't anymore. I don't like her yet, but I don't hate her either. She needs God worse than I did."

A large roar echoed through the stadium, and the Madison Musketeer Band blasted their victory song.

"Hey, we just scored!" Skye said. The girls started walking again. "You've got to admit we were, like, total losers. But the Chambers never trashed us. Neither did God. I think we ought to be praying for your mom more than ever."

"I'm praying as hard as I can," Sooze added. Then suddenly pointing to the back of the bleachers, she yelled out, "There's Jason!"

Skye held back. "Come on. Let's go find the other kids."

"One moment," Sooze said, forcing her body to move at a pace she had not been able to muster for some time.

"Unreal," Skye grumbled, trailing after Sooze, who hurried into Jason's shadow.

Jason's orange and green hair stuck out like it had frozen that way. Each ear had a lineup of three earrings. Despite the cold, his scrawny body was clad in only a short-sleeved black T-shirt and baggy cargo pants that bunched on the ground.

"Sooze, babe. Good to see you. What can I get for you tonight?" Jason's smile flashed with eagerness as his hands slipped into his pockets. "I've got any little thing your heart desires." Skye grabbed Sooze's coat sleeve. "Sooze, let's go."

"Wait!" Sooze said sharply. "I want to see what he's got."

"Sooze!" Skye said double sharply.

"I said wait a minute!"

"Yeah, what's the hurry, gorgeous?" Jason sneered. "We're just ready to start the party!"

"Not me! Not this time!" Skye said, turning. "I'll wait for you over there by the fence."

The snow had been falling in buckets; now it was falling by the truckloads. Skye had just barely turned toward the bleachers and now strained to see past the onslaught of flakes. "Sooze, don't do this!" Skye said, scarcely aware that she had just started a conversation with herself. "You'll be sorry."

By now the frigid air ran through Skye's veins like ice water. The snow quickly formed a thin blanket on the field, adding a chill that made Skye feel like she was standing on an iceberg. Skye wished she were home. She moved her feet and wiggled her toes, trying to get them warm.

"Come on, Sooze!" she grumbled. "I bet that dumb football would listen before you would."

The words flying between Jason and Sooze lasted longer than Skye thought *she* could. But, strangely, Skye noticed that nothing else passed between them. In fact, Sooze's hands never left her pockets. Finally, Sooze left Jason standing alone, scratching his head of frozen stiff hair.

"I told him to chill out," Sooze labored to say as she joined Skye. She let out a slight giggle. "Hey, get it? Snow, cold, chill? Anyway, I don't need that stuff anymore. Not since I've got God on my side."

Despite the cold, Skye managed a relieved smile. "I was afraid—"

"Yeah, I know," Sooze said. "C'mon, let's go find our *real* friends." They slowly walked away.

A thunderous cheer erupted from the Madison crowd, and the band played their victory march one more time. But Skye and Sooze had other things on their minds.

chapter fourteen

I never thought about buying gifts for anyone but me." Sooze forced her words out as she and Morgan maneuvered their wheelchairs through the crowded mall. For a month now, Sooze had begun to use her own wheelchair when she had to travel a considerable distance. "Christmas was always just an excuse for Mom to party. The rest of the family never bothered with us much, so holidays were no big deal. My brother Chuck and I usually just watched TV or ran around. I guess my running-around days are over."

Skye followed closely, making sure that their three winter coats and the packages in the girls' baskets stayed put.

"Wait a sec, you two," Skye said, saving a bag from tumbling to the floor. "I need to fix some things back here. Pull over. This place is packed. It's a miracle that you two haven't mowed down some poor shopper along the way."

After Skye had rearranged the cargo, the wheelchairs resumed, crawling like a pair of gigantic snails, trying their best to avoid distracted shoppers. Skye trailed behind and tried to balance bags that still had a mind of their own.

"Your running-around days might be over, but not your *running-over* days," Skye said.

"I have enough to worry about without being sued for reckless driving!" Sooze managed a giggle. "We just have to be extra careful, or some kid could lose his toes. Right, Morgan?"

"Right!" Morgan spun her chair around and took a long look at the line of stores on the other side of the mall. "I just love Christmas! What are you two buying Mr. and Mrs. C? It's only a few weeks until the big day!"

Excitement over celebrating her first Christmas as a Christian had Skye practically jumping out of her skin, especially the part about buying gifts for people she loved.

"I've noticed Mom's Bible is pretty ragged," Skye said. "I think I'll get her a new one—I'm thinking something fancy with a burgundy leather cover."

"How about Mr. C?" Morgan asked.

"Wait till you hear this! I saw the neatest little mustache grooming kit. It's perfect."

Sooze adjusted the baseball cap that covered her wig. "I was thinking about a sentimental gift for Mr. C. I thought maybe a new key chain with his initials, and a crazy visor for the new truck would be cool. Kind of a belated 'I'm really sorry for wrecking your truck' gift. What do you think?"

Skye studied her friend's eyes that betrayed tiredness and persistent pain. "Sooze, you okay? We can go now if you're too tired."

"Not a chance," Sooze answered. "I've got to find a bright blue scarf for Mrs. C. to go with her western duds."

"Brilliant," Morgan said, brushing back her hair. "I've been saving for months for what I'd like to get them. Did you know their twentieth anniversary is next month?

I saw the neatest wall clock with tiny running horses on it. They'll love it."

Skye thought of something special she had seen in a store the week before, and her heart played leap frog. *That's right!*

"Hey, now that we're talking horses, I know something we could all get them, and it wouldn't cost us megabucks. Off to the toy store!"

Sooze scrunched her face like she was sucking lemons. "The toy store?"

Morgan laughed. "Okay, Skye, if you say so. But I'm guessing you've lost your mind."

"Stay with me. You'll see!" Skye promised.

The girls giggled their way to the other end of the mall, excused themselves past other shoppers, and finally approached the window of the Just Kidding toy store.

"Look at those!" Skye bubbled as they lined up in front of the store window—horse models of all shapes and sizes posed in prances or rearing on their hind legs. The horses stood around a red barn on a green grass-like carpet, and a small white fence encircled the entire display. Above the exquisite models hung a wooden plaque carved with the word *BREYER*.

"Wow!" Morgan said as she stared at the display. "I've seen some of these horses before, but never in a spread like this!"

"This is awesome!" Sooze said.

"Check it out," Skye said, her voice rising to a higher pitch. "There's one in there for every horse at Keystone. Look—there in the back on the left. That one's just like Champ!"

Sooze pointed to another corner. "Hey, there's Blaze! Look, Morgan, its legs are black just like hers!"

Morgan leaned forward in her chair. "Yeah, I see it. Do you see Pepsi anywhere?"

"Yeah," Skye answered, "next to the black stallion. If I didn't know better, I would've thought they used Pepsi's picture to make that horse. It looks like her twin."

"This is too sweet," Sooze said, as she thought her days of riding Pepsi. "Oh, I get it, Skye."

"Me too," Morgan added.

Skye's whole face sparkled with a smile. "It won't cost that much if we all pool our money. We could get both Mom and Dad a model of their horse. Over there in the right corner is Chief. Do you see him?"

"Yep," Sooze said.

"Unreal," Morgan said. "That model is even the same pinto colors as Chief. They'll love these! Let's do it."

Sooze backed away from the window and bowed her head. Her swollen fingers played with each other.

Skye followed Sooze's reaction. "What's the matter?"

"Do you feel sick?" Morgan added.

Sooze looked up and stared at the window. "Nah, nothing like that. Since I'm not getting chemo, I'm not sick anymore. Just tired. I told you before I never bought a gift for anybody in my whole life. That includes my mother. Not for any reason. Not even her birthday. She collects things like this. You should see our one bedroom upstairs. She has ceramics and dolls and plastic animals sitting all over the place. I bet she'd like one of these. I could get her the one that looks like Pepsi."

"How could she not love it? That's a super idea," Skye said.

Morgan turned her chair toward the entrance. "C'mon," she said, with a smile as big as Skye's, "let's go shop!"

The busy weeks before Christmas brought the sights and smells that heralded the joy of the long-awaited holiday.

Shade Valley now glistened with several inches of snow, adding to the season's delight. The spirit of giving to honor Christ's birth seemed to reach even into the darkest corners of every home, igniting them with lights of hope displayed in brilliant color. Yet the beauty of the Christmas season somehow sent a more somber message to the family at Keystone Stables. Though prayers for Sooze had been going up constantly, it had become too clear that five months of treatments were not helping Sooze. She was gravely ill.

Shortly after the girls' shopping trip, Sooze's physical condition weakened so fast that she was no longer able even to sit up. Mr. and Mrs. Chambers had stationed a hospital bed for her in their living room where a fresh towering spruce tree twinkled in one corner. White lights around the bay window cast a soft glow in the room and on the snow-covered shrubs outside.

Skye's and Morgan's spare moments always brought them to their friend whom they had grown to love. Every evening they ate their meals at her bedside, encouraging her, relating the news of the day, telling her about the horses, reading to her from the Bible, and praying with her before she fell asleep. Sooze grew weaker and thinner. Much of the time, her medication kept her in a deep sleep. When she was awake, it took all her strength to manage a few words. But she could smile, and when she did, it illuminated her entire face.

On Christmas Eve, snowflakes fell on an already sparkling winter wonderland. Skye and Mr. Chambers had finished their barn chores, and Mrs. Chambers and Morgan had just done the dishes when Pastor Newman stopped by.

The family gathered around Sooze's bed and sang Christmas carols. After Pastor Newman prayed and left, Skye and Morgan decided to wrap the last few gifts at the dining room table. Mr. and Mrs. Chambers reclaimed their chairs next to Sooze. A Christmas CD played softly in the background as the scent of cinnamon wafted through the air.

Skye wrapped gold ribbon around a shiny green package. Her head throbbed from endless crying, and her throat ached. *I know God does miracles. He healed Dad*, she told herself. *And he just has to do another miracle now.*

"Do you think God could heal her?" Skye asked Morgan. "I mean, she's been fighting so hard."

"I don't know what to say," Morgan replied as she taped a box shut. "Mrs. C. says that God's ways are not our ways."

"It doesn't even seem like Christmas, does it?" Skye felt her throat tighten again and her eyes tear up. "I mean, how can we be happy at a time like this?"

Morgan pushed the box she was wrapping to the center of the table. "I know. This is the worst thing I've ever gone through."

"I just don't get it." Skye looked up into Morgan's glistening eyes.

"Skye, can't you see that God sent Sooze here so she would come to know him? She's going to a far better place than we can even imagine. She's going where it's Christmas every day!"

"Yeah, I know, but it's still hard. She was just getting her act together and really enjoying Pepsi. I'll never forget when we talked at Piney Hollow the night of the retreat. She really did come clean. And even the way she felt about her mom changed. She's been praying for her too."

"Yeah, I know." Morgan sighed and reached for the box again. "Just remember, we promised that we'd pray for her mom too. God can change her heart."

"Yeah, but when? Can you believe Mrs. Bodmer hasn't come even once to see Sooze? I wonder if she even cares one little bit."

"Some people just can't handle being around sick folks. Like my family," said Morgan. "It's too scary for them. Like I said, we'll just keep praying."

"Girls." Skye heard Mrs. Chambers' voice from the living room. "You better come in here."

Skye and Morgan looked into each other's eyes. Neither one said what Skye knew was in each of their hearts. It was time to say good-bye. But as they slipped into the room, they noticed that Sooze was awake. A weak smile crossed her face as she caught sight of her friends.

Mr. and Mrs. Chambers were on each side of the bed. Their eyes were swollen and red; both of them looked like they hadn't slept in a week. Mrs. Chambers stroked Sooze's cheek gently. On a lamp table next to the bed rested a gift box with a tag labeled "Mom." A silence settled on the group, and then Sooze spoke. "She's coming. I know she is. God told me my mom is coming to say good-bye."

Skye gave Morgan a quick look and then turned her eyes back to Sooze. In only a few days, it seemed that Sooze had faded away to almost nothing. Her head, covered with a thin layer of fuzz, highlighted her eyes that had sunken deeper into her ashen face. Her chest rose with each shallow breath and then lowered in a jerking motion.

Skye sat, staring at her friend. *This can't be real. I've got to wake up from this nightmare,* she told herself. The heaviest weight she had ever felt pressed down on her. It felt like her heart was being ripped right out of her chest. *My best friend is dying, and I can't do a thing to help her.* Skye blinked, streams of hot tears flooding her cheeks. With a sigh of disbelief, she leaned on the bed and folded her hands in front of her quivering lips.

A knock at the door, faint and unsure, broke the tearful silence. Mrs. Chambers brushed the tears from her face and turned toward the gentle knock. She went to the door and slowly opened it.

As Mrs. Chambers stood back for the guest to enter, Skye and Morgan both gasped. There before them stood a lonely figure, cold as the rush of the winter night itself.

Mrs. Chambers reached out to welcome the woman at the door, and Skye's heart leaped. She brushed back her tears and as she did, a deep inner peace made its way into the depths of her soul, a peace that only comes from God.

"Mrs. Bodmer, come in!" Mr. Chambers said.

With a newfound hope in her heart, Skye turned to Sooze, who had turned her head toward her mother.

"Oh, Sooze," Skye said with excitement. "Your mother did come. Now I know God answers prayer."

Sooze smiled, and Skye thought she looked like an angel. Sooze reached out one thin, pale arm to the woman who now stood next to her bed.

Mrs. Bodmer kissed her daughter's hand as tears flowed freely from her eyes onto the bed covers.

"I love you, Mom," Sooze said.

"I know I haven't ever told you, Sooze, but I love you too. I don't know why I couldn't ever do right by you. I'm so sorry. Can you ever forgive me?"

Sooze nodded sweetly and continued to smile up into her mother's face. "I forgive you, and God will forgive you too, Mom. All you have to do is ask."

A comforting presence filled the room that, without question in Skye's heart, outshone the glow of the Christmas lights. She knew God was here. She knew there was nothing to fear.

Slowly, mustering strength from a source higher than her own, Sooze stared fixedly at the corner of the room.

"It's time for me to go now. I'm not afraid. I'll see you all again in heaven one day."

Sooze's voice was barely more than a whisper. Her lungs emptied with one long rattle, and her eyes drooped shut. Her parched lips forced upward into her last smile on Earth, one that could only mean victory!

For the next few moments, which seemed like hours, the family sat in frozen silence, hoping against hope that they might see one more breath.

Mr. Chambers' weak voice cracked. "Sooze is with the Lord."

Skye sat with her family. Their sobs intermingled with the fleeting joy of a Christmas Eve that would stay with them the rest of their lives. Mrs. Chambers stood with her arms encircling Mrs. Bodmer, comforting her. Finally, Mr. Chambers prayed, committing Sooze and their own futures into the hands of the Lord.

Someday, Skye's breaking heart declared with its own victorious shout, *someday in heaven, we'll be together again!*

And now clearer than ever, the message of the season rang out—that Jesus Christ came to Earth that first Christmas so long ago for just this purpose—to take away the power of death.

Quietly at first, and then with gathering strength, the family began to sing *Silent Night* as a hymn of praise to God.

A Letter to my Keystone Stables Fans

Dear Reader,

Are you crazy about horses like I am? Are you fortunate enough to have a horse now, or are you dreaming about the day when you will have one of your very own?

I've been crazy about horses ever since I can remember. When I was a child, I lived where I couldn't have a horse. Even if I had lived in the country, my folks didn't have the money to buy me one. So, as I grew up in a small coal town in central Pennsylvania, I dreamed about horses and collected horse pictures and horse models. I drew horse pictures and wrote horse stories, and I read every horse book I could get my hands on.

For Christmas when I was ten, I received a leather-fringed western jacket and a cowgirl hat. Weather permitting, I wore them when I walked to and from school. On the way, I imagined that I was riding a gleaming white steed into a world of mountain trails and forest paths.

Occasionally, during the summer, my mother took me to a riding academy where I rode a horse for one hour.

at a time. I always rubbed my hands (and hard!) on my mount before we left the ranch. For the rest of the day I tried not to wash my hands so I could smell the horse and remember the great time I had. Of course, I never could sit at the dinner table without Mother first sending me to the faucet to get rid of that "awful stench."

To get my own horse, I had to wait until I grew up, married, and bought a home in the country with enough land for a barn and a pasture. Moon Doggie, my very first horse, was a handsome brown and white pinto Welsh Mountain Pony. Many other equines came to live at our place where, in later years, my husband and I also opened our hearts to foster kids who needed a caring home. Most of the kids loved the horses as much as I did.

Although owning horses and rearing foster kids are now in my past, I fondly remember my favorite steed, who has long since passed from the scene. Rex, part Quarter Horse and part Tennessee Walker, was a 14 ½ hands-high bay. Rex was the kind of horse every kid dreams about. With a smooth walking gait, he gave me a thrilling ride every time I climbed into the saddle. Yet, he was so gentle a young child could sit confidently on his back. Rex loved sugar cubes and nuzzled my pockets to find them. When cleaning his hooves, all I had to do was touch the target leg, and he lifted his hoof into my waiting hands. Rex was my special horse, and although he died at the ripe old age of twenty-five many years ago, I still miss him.

If you have a horse now or just dream about the day when you will, I beg you to do all you can to learn how to treat with tender love and respect one of God's most beautiful creatures. Horses make wonderful pets, but they require much more attention than a dog or a cat. For their loyal devotion to you, they only ask that you love them in return with the proper food, a clean barn, and the best of care.

Rex

Although Skye and Champ's story that you just read is fiction, the following pages contain horse facts that any horse lover will enjoy. It is my desire that these pages will help you to either care for your own horse better now or prepare you for that moment when you'll be able to throw your arms around that one special horse of your dreams that you can call your very own.

Happy riding!
Marsha Hubler

Are You Ready to Own Your First Horse?

The most exciting moment in any horse lover's life is to look into the eyes of a horse she can call her very own. No matter how old you are when you buy your first horse, it's hard to match the thrill of climbing onto his back and taking that first ride on a woodsy trail or dusty road that winds through open fields. A well-trained mount will give you a special friendship and years of pleasure as you learn to work with him and become a confident equestrian team.

But owning a horse involves much more than hopping on his back, racing him into a lather of sweat, and putting him back in his stall until you're ready to ride him again.

If you have your own horse now, you've already realized that caring for a horse takes a great amount of time and money. Besides feeding him twice a day, you must also groom him, clean his stall, "pick" his hooves, and have a farrier (a horseshoe maker and applier) and veterinarian make regular visits.

If you don't own a horse and you are begging your parents to buy one, please realize that you can't keep the horse in your garage and just feed him grass cuttings left over from a mowed lawn. It is a sad fact that too many neglected horses have ended up in rescue shelters after well-meaning families did not know how to properly care for their steeds.

If you feel that you are ready to have your own horse, please take time to answer the following questions. If you say yes to all of them, then you are well on your way to being the proud owner of your very own mount:

1. Do you have the money to purchase:
   - the horse? (A good grade horse can start at $800. Registered breeds can run into the thousands.)
   - a saddle, pad, and bridle, and a winter blanket or raincoat? ($300+ brand new)
   - a hard hat (helmet) and riding boots? ($150+)
   - essentials such as coat and hoof conditioner, bug repellent, electric clipper and grooming kit, saddle soap, First Aid kit, and vitamins? ($150+)

2. Does your family own at least a one-stall shed or barn and at least two acres of grass (enough pasture for one horse) to provide adequate grazing for your horse during warm months? If not, do you have the money to regularly purchase quality oats and alfalfa/timothy hay, and do you have the place to store the hay? Oh, and let's not forget the constant supply of sawdust or straw you need for stall bedding!

3. Are you ready to get up early enough every day to give your horse a bucket of fresh water, feed him a coffee can full of oats and one or two sections of clean dry hay (if you have no pasture), and "muck out" the manure from the barn?

4. Every evening, are you again ready to water and feed your horse, clean the barn, groom him, and pick his hooves?
5. Will you ride him at least twice a week, weather permitting?
6. If the answer to any of the above questions is no, then does your family have the money to purchase a horse and board him at a nearby stable? (Boarding fees can run as high as a car payment. Ask your parents how much that is.)

So, there you have the bare facts about owning and caring for a horse. If you don't have your own horse yet, perhaps you'll do as I did when I was young: I read all the books I could about horses. I analyzed all the facts about the money and care needed to make a horse happy. Sad as it made me feel, I finally realized that I would have to wait until I was much older to assume such a great responsibility. And now years later, I can look back and say, "For the horse's sake, I'm very glad I did wait."

I hope you've made the decision to give your horse the best possible TLC that you can. That might mean improving his care now or waiting until you're older to get a horse of your own. Whatever you and your parents decide, please remember that the result of your efforts should be a happy horse. If that's the case, you will be happy too.

Let's Go Horse Shopping!

If you are like I was when I was younger, I dreamed of owning the most beautiful horse in the world. My dream horse, with his long-flowing mane and wavy tail dragging on the ground, would arch his neck and prance with only a touch of my hand on his withers or a gentle rub of my boot heel on his barrel. My dream horse was often different colors. Sometimes he was silvery white; other times he was jet black. He was often a pinto blend of the deepest chocolate browns, blacks, and whites. No matter what color he was, he always took me on a perfect ride, responding to my slightest commands.

When I was old enough to be responsible to care for my own steed, I already knew that the horse of my dreams was just that, the horse of my dreams. To own a prancing pure white stallion or a high-stepping coal-black mare, I would have to buy a Lipizzaner, American Saddle Horse, or an Andalusian. But those kinds of horses were either not for sale to a beginner with a tiny barn or they cost so much, I couldn't afford one. I was amazed to discover that there are about 350 different breeds of horses, and I had to look for a horse that was just right for me, possibly even a good grade horse (that means not registered) that was a safe mount. Color really didn't matter as long as the horse was healthy and gave a safe, comfortable ride. (But I'm not sure what my friends might have said if I had a purple horse. That certainly would have been a "horse of a different color!") Then I had to decide if I wanted to ride western or English style. Well, living in central Pennsylvania farm country with oodles of trails and dirt roads, the choice for me was simple: western.

I'm sure if you don't have your own horse yet, you've dreamed and thought a lot about what your first horse will be. Perhaps you've already had a horse, but now you're thinking of buying another one. What kind should you get?

Let's look at some of the breeds that are the most popular for both western and English riders today. We'll briefly trace a few breeds' roots and characteristics while you decide if that kind of horse might be the one for you. Please keep in mind that this information speaks to generalities of the breeds. If given the proper care and training, most any breeds of horses makes excellent mounts as well.

Some Popular Breeds (Based on Body Confirmation)

The Arabian

Sometimes called "The China Doll of the Horse Kingdom," the Arabian is known as the most beautiful of horse breeds because of its delicate features. Although research indicates Arabians are the world's oldest and purest breed, it is not known whether they originated in Arabia. However, many Bible scholars believe that the first horse that God created in the Garden of Eden must have embodied the strength and beauty that we see in the Arabian horse of today. It is also believed that all other breeds descended from this gorgeous breed that has stamina as well as courage and intelligence.

A purebred Arabian has a height of only 14 or 15 hands, a graceful arch in his neck, and a high carriage in his tail. It is easy to identify one of these horses by examining his head. If you see a small, delicate "dish" face with a broad forehead and tiny muzzle, two ears that point inward and large eyes that are often ringed in black, you are probably looking at an Arabian. The breed comes in all colors, (including dappled and some paint), but if you run your finger against the grain of any pureblood Arabian's coat, you will see an underlying bed of black skin. Perhaps that's why whites are often called "grays."

Generally, Arabians are labeled spirited and skittish, even though they might have been well trained. If you have your heart set on buying an Arabian, make sure you first have the experience to handle a horse that, although he might be loyal, will also want to run with the wind.

The Morgan

The Morgan horse, like a Quarter Horse (see below), can explode into a gallop for a short distance. The Morgan, with its short legs, muscles, and fox ears, also looks very much like the Quarter Horse. How can we tell the two breeds apart?

A Morgan is chunkier than a Quarter Horse, especially in his stout neck. His long, wavy tail often flows to the ground. His trot is quick and short and with such great stamina, he can trot all day long.

So where are the Morgan's roots?

The horse breed was named after Justin Morgan, a frail music teacher, who lived in Vermont at the turn of the eighteenth century. Instead of receiving cash for a debt owed, Mr. Morgan was given two colts. The smallest one, which he called Figure, was an undersized dark bay with a black mane and tail. Mr. Morgan sold the one colt, but he kept Figure, which he thought was a cross between a Thoroughbred and an Arabian. Over the years, he found the horse to be strong enough to pull logs and fast enough to beat Thoroughbreds in one afternoon and eager to do it all over again the same day!

When Mr. Morgan died, his short but powerful horse was called "Justin Morgan" in honor of his owner. After that, all of Justin Morgan's foals were called Morgans. The first volume of the Morgan Horse Register was published in 1894. Since then, hundreds of thousands of Morgans have been registered.

If you go Morgan hunting, you will find the breed in any combination of blacks, browns, and whites. Don't look for a tall horse because all Morgans are between 14 and 15 hands tall, just right for beginners. If you're fortunate enough to find a well-trained Morgan, he'll give you years of pleasure whether you ask him to gallop down a country trail, pull a wagon, or learn to jump obstacles.

The Mustang

If you want a taste of America's Wild West from days gone by, then you should treat yourself to the "Wild Horse of America," the Mustang.

This 14–15 hand, stout horse has its roots from Cortez and the Spanish conquistadors from the sixteenth century.

Although the Mustang's name comes from the Spanish word, *mesteno*, which means "a stray or wild grazer," he is most well known as the horse of the Native Americans. Numerous tribes all over the western plains captured horses that had escaped from their Spanish owners and ran wild. The Native Americans immediately claimed the Mustang as a gift from their gods and showed the world that the horse was, and is, easy to train once domesticated.

It didn't take long for the white settlers to discover the versatility of the Mustang. Because of his endurance, this little horse soon became a favorite for the Pony Express, the U.S. cavalry, cattle round-ups, and caravans.

Since the 1970s, the U.S. Bureau of Land Management has stepped in to save the Mustangs from extinction. As a result, herds of Mustangs still roam freely in U.S. western plains today. At different times of the year and in different parts of the country, the Adopt-a-Horse-or-Burro Program allows horse lovers to take a Mustang or burro home for a year and train it to be a reliable mount. After the year, the eligible family can receive a permanent ownership title from the government. As of October 2007, more than 218,000 wild horses and burros have been placed into private care since the adoption program began in 1973.

If you'd like a "different" kind of horse that sometimes has a scrubby look but performs with the fire of the arab-barb blood, then go shopping for a Mustang. You'll find him in any black, brown, or white combination and with the determination and stamina to become your best equine friend.

The Quarter Horse

There's no horse lover anywhere in the world who hasn't heard of the American Quarter Horse. In fact, the Quarter Horse is probably the most popular breed in the United States today.

But what exactly is a Quarter Horse? Is he only a quarter of a horse in size, therefore, just a pony? No, this fantastic breed isn't a quarter of anything!

The Quarter Horse originated in American colonial times in Virginia when European settlers bred their stout English workhorses with the Native Americans' Mustangs. The result? A short-legged but muscular equine with a broad head and little "fox" ears, a horse that has great strength and speed.

It didn't take long for the colonists and Native Americans to discover that their new crossbreed was the fastest piece of horseflesh in the world for a quarter of a mile. Thus, the breed was christened the American Quarter Horse and began to flourish. Besides running quick races, it also pulled wagons, canal boats, and plows. When the American West opened up, cowpokes discovered that the Quarter Horse was perfect for herding cattle and to help rope steers. Although it remained a distinct breed for over three hundred years in the U.S., the Quarter Horse was only recognized with its own studbook in 1941.

If you are looking for a reliable mount that has a comfortable trot and smooth gallop, you might want to look at some *seasoned* Quarter Horses. (That means they have been trained properly and are at least five or six years old.) They come in any color or combination of colors. Their temperament is generally friendly, yet determined to get the job done that you ask them to do.

The Shetland Pony

Many beginning riders incorrectly believe that the smaller the horse, the easier it is to control him. You might be thinking, "I'm tiny, so I need a tiny horse!" But many beginners have found out the hard way that a Shetland Pony is sometimes no piece of cake.

Shetland Ponies originated as far back as the Bronze Age in the Shetland Isles, northeast of mainland Scotland. Research has found that they are related to the ancient Scandinavian ponies. Shetland Ponies were first used for pulling carts, carrying peat and other items, and plowing farmland. Thousands of Shetlands also worked as "pit ponies," pulling coal carts in British mines in the mid–nineteenth century. The Shetland found its way at the same time to the United States when they were imported to also work in mines.

The American Shetland Pony Club was founded in 1888 as a registry to keep the pedigrees for all the Shetlands that were being imported from Europe at that time.

Shetlands are usually only 10.2 hands or shorter. They have a small head, sometimes with a dished face, big Bambi eyes, and small ears. The original breed has a short, muscular neck, stocky bodies, and short, strong legs. Shetlands can give you a bouncy ride because of their short broad backs and deep girths. These ponies have long thick manes and tails, and in winter climates their coats of any color can grow long and fuzzy.

If you decide you'd like to own a Shetland, spend a great deal of time looking for one that is mild mannered. Because of past years of hard labor, the breed now shows a dogged determination that often translates into stubbornness. So be careful, and don't fall for that sweet, fuzzy face without riding the pony several times before you buy him. You might get a wild, crazy ride from a "shortstuff" mount that you never bargained for!

The Tennessee Walking Horse

If you buy a Tennessee Walker, get ready for a thrilling ride as smooth as running water!

The Tennessee Walking Horse finds its roots in 1886 in Tennessee, when a Standardbred (a Morgan and

Standardbred trotter cross) stallion named Black Allan refused to trot; instead, he chose to amble or "walk" fast. With effortless speed comparable to other horses' trots, Black Allan's new gait (each hoof hitting the ground at a different time) amazed the horse world. Owners of Thoroughbreds and saddle horses were quick to breed their mares to this delightful new "rocking-horse" stud, and the Tennessee Walker was on its way to becoming one of the most popular breeds in the world. In just a few short years, the Walker became the favorite mount of not only circuit-riding preachers and plantation owners, but ladies riding sidesaddle as well.

Today the Walker, which comes in any black, brown, or white color or combination, is a versatile horse and is comfortable when ridden English or western. He is usually 15 to 17 hands tall and has a long neck and sloping shoulders. His head is large but refined, and he has small ears. Because he has a short back, his running walk, for which he is known, comes naturally.

If you go shopping for a Tennesee Walker, you will find a horse that is usually mild mannered yet raring to go. Although most Walkers are big and you might need a stepstool to climb on one, you will be amazed at how smooth his walk and rocking-horse canter is. In fact, you might have trouble making yourself get off!

Some Popular Breeds (Based on Body Color)

The Appaloosa

French cave paintings thousands of years old have "spotted" horses among its subjects, ancient China had labeled their spotted horses as "heavenly," and Persians have called their spotted steeds "sacred." Yet the spotted Appaloosa breed that we know today is believed to have originated in the northwestern Native Americans tribe called the Nez Perce in the seventeenth century.

When colonists expanded the United States territory westward, they found a unique people who lived near the Palouse River (which runs from north central Idaho to the Snake River in southeast Washington State). The Nez Perce Indian tribe had bred a unique horse—red or blue roans with white spots on the rump. Fascinated, the colonists called the beautiful breed *palousey*, which means "the stream of the green meadows." Gradually, the name changed to *Appaloosa*.

The Nez Perce people lost most of their horses following the end of the Nez Perce War in 1877, and the breed started to decline for several decades. However, a small number of dedicated Appaloosa lovers kept the breed alive. Finally, a breed registry was formed in 1938. The Appaloosa was named the official state horse of Idaho in 1975.

If you decide to buy an Appaloosa, you'll own one of the most popular breeds in the United States today. It is best known as a stock horse used in a number of western riding events, but it's also seen in many other types of equestrian contests as well. So if you would like to ride English or western, or want to show your horse or ride him on a mountain trail, an Appaloosa could be just the horse for you.

Appaloosas can be any solid base color, but the gorgeous blanket of spots that sometimes cover the entire horse identifies the special breed. Those spotted markings are not the same as pintos or the "dapple grays" and some other horse colors. For a horse to be registered as a pureblood Appaloosa, it also has to have striped hooves, white outer coat (sclera) encircling its brown or blue eyes, and mottled (spotted) skin around the eyes and lips. The Appaloosa is one of the few breeds to have skin mottling, and so this characteristic is a surefire way of identifying a true member of the breed.

In 1983, the Appaloosa Horse Club in America decided to limit the crossbreeding of Appaloosas to only three main confirmation breeds: the Arabian, the American Quarter horse, and the Thoroughbred. Thus, the Appaloosa color breed also became a true confirmation breed as well.

If you want your neighbors to turn their heads your way when you ride past, then look for a well-trained Appaloosa. Most registered "Apps" are 15 hands or shorter but are full of muscle and loaded with spots. Sometimes, though, it takes several years for an Appaloosa's coat to mature to its full color. So if it's color you're looking for, shop for a seasoned App!

The Pinto

The American Pinto breed has its origins in the wild Mustang of the western plains. The seventeenth and eighteenth century Native Americans bred color into their "ponies," using them for warhorses and prizing those with the richest colors. When the "Westward Ho" pioneers captured wild Mustangs with flashy colors, they bred them to all different breeds of European stock horses. Thus, the Pinto has emerged as a color breed, which includes all different body shapes and sizes today.

The Pinto Horse Association of America was formed in 1956, although the bloodlines of many Pintos can be traced three or four generations before then. The association doesn't register Appaloosas, draft breeds, or horses with mule roots or characteristics. Today more than 100,000 Pintos are registered throughout the U.S., Canada, Europe, and Asia.

Pintos have a dark background with random patches of white and have two predominant color patterns:

1. Tobiano (Toe-bee-ah'-no) Pintos are white with large spots of brown or black color. Spots can cover much of the head, chest, flank, and rump, often including the tail. Legs are generally white,

which makes the horse look like he's white with flowing spots of color. The white usually crosses the center of the back of the horse.

2. Overo (O-vair'-o) Pintos are colored horses with jagged white markings that originate on the animal's side or belly and spread toward the neck, tail, legs, and back. The deep, rich browns or blacks appear to frame the white. Thus, Overos often have dark backs and dark legs. Horses with bald or white faces are often Overos. Their splashy white markings on the rest of their body make round, lacy patterns.

Perhaps you've heard the term *paint* and wonder if that kind of horse is the same as a Pinto. Well, amazingly, the two are different breeds! A true Paint horse (registered by the American Paint Horse Association) must be bred from pureblood Paints, Quarter Horses, or Thoroughbreds. The difference in eligibility between the two registries has to do with the bloodlines of the horse, not its color or pattern.

So if you're shopping for a flashy mount and you don't care about a specific body type of horse, then set your sites on a Pinto or Paint. You might just find a well-trained registered or grade horse that has the crazy colors you've been dreaming about for a very long time!

The Palomino

No other color of horse will turn heads his way than the gorgeous golden Palomino. While the average person thinks the ideal color for a Palomino is like a shiny gold coin, the Palomino breed's registry allows all kinds of coat colors as long as the mane and tail are silvery white. A white blaze can be on the face but can't extend beyond the eyes. The Palomino can also have white stockings, but the white can't extend beyond the knees. Colors of

Palominos can range from a deep, dark chocolate to an almost-white cremello. As far as body confirmation, four breeds are strongly represented in crossbreeding with the palomino today: the American Saddlebred, Tennessee Walker, Morgan, and Quarter Horse.

No one is sure where the Palomino came from, but it is believed that the horse came from Spain. An old legend says that Isabella, queen of Spain in the late fifteenth century, loved her golden horses so much she sent one stallion and five mares across the Atlantic to start thriving in the New World. Eventually those six horses lived in what is now Texas and New Mexico, where Native Americans captured the horses' offspring and incorporated them into their daily lives. From those six horses came all the Palominos in the United States, which proves how adaptable the breed is in different climates.

Today you can find Palominos all over the world and involved in all kinds of settings from jumping to ranching to rodeos. One of their most popular venues is pleasing crowds in parades, namely the Tournament of Roses Parade in Pasadena, California, every New Year's Day.

Perhaps you've dreamed of owning a horse that you could be proud of whether you are trail riding on a dirt road, showing in a Western Pleasure Class, or strutting to the beat of a band in a parade. If that's the case, then the Palomino is the horse for you!

If you're shopping for the best in bloodlines, look for a horse that has a double registry! With papers that show the proper bloodlines, an Appaloosa Quarter Horse can be double registered. Perhaps you'd like a Palomino Morgan or a Pinto Tennessee Walker?

Who Can Ride a Horse?

As you have read this book about Skye, Morgan, and some of the other children with special needs, perhaps you could identify with one in particular. Do you have what society calls a handicap or disability? Do you use a wheelchair? Do you have any friends who are blind or have autism? Do you or your friends with special needs believe that none of you could ever ride a horse?

Although Keystone Stables is a fictitious place, there are real ranches and camps that connect horses with children just like Skye and Morgan, Sooze in book two, Tanya in book three, Jonathan in book four, Katie in book five, Joey in book six, and Wanda in book seven. That special kind of treatment and interaction has a long complicated name called Equine Facilitated Psychotherapy (EFP.)

EFP might include handling and grooming the horse, lunging, riding, or driving a horse-drawn cart. In an EFP program, a licensed mental health professional works together with a certified horse handler. Sometimes one EFP person can have the credentials for both. Whatever the case, the professionals are dedicated to helping both the child and the horse learn to work together as a team.

Children with autism benefit greatly because of therapeutic riding. Sometimes a child who has never been able to speak or "connect" with another person, even a parent, will bond with a horse in such a way that the child learns to relate to other people or starts to talk.

An author friend has told me of some of her family members who've had experience with horses and autistic children. They tell a story about a mute eight-year-old boy who was taking therapeutic treatment. One day as he was riding a well-trained mount that knew just what to do, the horse stopped for no reason and refused to budge. The leader said, "Walk on" and pulled on the halter, but the horse wouldn't move. The sidewalkers (people who help the child balance in the saddle) all did the same thing with the same result. Finally, the little boy who was still sitting on the horse shouted, "Walk on, Horsie!" The horse immediately obeyed.

So the good news for some horse-loving children who have serious health issues is that they might be able to work with horses. Many kids like Morgan, who has cerebral palsy, and blind Katie (book five) actually can learn to ride! That's because all over the world, people who love horses and children have started therapy riding academies to teach children with special needs how to ride and/or care for a horse. Highly trained horses and special equipment like high-backed saddles with Velcro strips on the fenders make it safe for kids with special needs to become skilled equestrians and thus learn to work with their own handicaps as they never have been able to do before!

A Word about Horse Whispering

If you are constantly reading about horses and know a lot about them, you probably have heard of horse whispering, something that many horse behaviorists do today to train horses. This training process is much different than what the majority of horsemen did several decades ago.

We've all read Wild West stories or seen movies in which the cowpoke "broke" a wild horse by climbing on his back and hanging on while the poor horse bucked until he was so exhausted he could hardly stand. What that type of training did was break the horse's spirit, and the horse learned to obey out of fear. Many "bronco busters" from the past also used whips, ropes, sharp spurs, and painful bits to make the horses respond, which they did only to avoid the pain the trainers caused.

Thankfully, the way many horses become reliable mounts has changed dramatically. Today many horses are trained, not broken. The trainer "communicates" with the horse using herd language. Thus, the horse bonds with his trainer quickly, looks to that person as his herd leader, and is ready to obey every command.

Thanks to Monty Roberts, the "man who listens to horses," and other professional horse whispering trainers like him, most raw or green horses (those that are just learning to respond to tack and a rider) are no longer broken.

Horses are now trained to accept the tack and rider in a short time with proven methods of horse whispering. Usually working in a round pen, the trainer begins by making large movements and noise as a predator would, encouraging the horse to run away. The trainer then gives the horse the choice to flee or bond. Through body language, the trainer asks the horse, "Will you choose me to be your herd leader and follow me?"

Often the horse responds with predictable herd behavior by twitching an ear toward his trainer then by lowering his head and licking to display an element of trust. The trainer mocks the horse's passive body language, turns his back on the horse, and, without eye contact, invites him to come closer. The bonding occurs when the horse chooses to be with the human and walks toward the trainer, thus accepting his leadership and protection.

Horse whispering has become one of the most acceptable, reliable, and humane ways to train horses. Today we have multitudes of rider-and-horse teams that have bonded in such a special way, both the rider and the horse enjoy each other's company. So when you're talking to your friends about horses, always remember to say the horses have been trained, not broken. The word *broken* is part of the horse's past and should remain there forever.

Bible Verses about Horses

Do you know there are about 150 verses in the Bible that include the word *horse*? It seems to me that if God mentioned horses so many times in the Bible, then he is very fond of one of his most beautiful creatures.

Some special verses about horses in the Bible make any horse lover want to shout. Look at this exciting passage from the book of Revelation that tells us about a wonderful time in the future:

"I saw heaven standing open and there before me was a white horse, whose rider is called Faithful and True. With justice he judges and makes war. His eyes are like blazing fire, and on his head are many crowns. He has a name written on him that no one knows but he himself. He is dressed in a robe dipped in blood, and his name is the Word of God. The armies of heaven were following him riding on white horses and dressed in fine linen, white and clean" (Revelation 19:11–14).

The rider who is faithful and true is the Lord Jesus Christ. The armies of heaven on white horses who follow Jesus are those who have accepted him as their Lord and Savior. I've accepted Christ, so I know that some day I'll get to ride a white horse in heaven. Do you think he will be a Lipizzaner, an Andalusian, or an Arabian? Maybe it will be a special new breed of white horses that God is preparing just for that special time.

Perhaps you never realized that there are horses in heaven. Perhaps you never thought about how you could go to heaven when you die. You can try to be as good as gold, but the Bible says that to go to heaven, you must ask Jesus to forgive your sins. Verses to think about: "For all have sinned and fall short of the glory of God" (Romans 3:23); "For God so loved the world that he gave his one and only son, that whoever believes in him shall not perish but have eternal life (John 3:16); "For everyone who calls on the name of the Lord will be saved" (Romans 10:13).

Do you want to be part of Jesus' cavalry in heaven some day? Have you ever asked Jesus to forgive your sins and make you ready for heaven? If you've never done so, please ask Jesus to save your soul today.

As I'm riding my prancing white steed with his long wavy mane and tail dragging to the ground, I'll be looking for you!

Glossary of Gaits

Gait—A gait is the manner of movement; the way a horse goes.

There are four natural or major gaits most horses use: walk, trot, canter, and gallop.

Walk—In the walk, the slowest gait, hooves strike the ground in a four-beat order: right hind hoof, right fore (or front) hoof, left hind hoof, left fore hoof.

Trot—In the trot, hooves strike the ground in diagonals in a one-two beat: right hind and left forefeet together, left hind and right forefeet together.

Canter—The canter is a three-beat gait containing an instant during which all four hooves are off the ground. The foreleg that lands last is called the *lead* leg and seems to point in the direction of the canter.

Gallop—The gallop is the fastest gait. If fast enough, it's a four-beat gait, with each hoof landing separately: right hind hoof, left hind hoof just before right fore hoof, left fore hoof.

Other gaits come naturally to certain breeds or are developed through careful breeding.

Running walk – This smooth gait comes naturally to the Tennessee walking horse. The horse glides between a walk and a trot.

Pace – A two-beat gait, similar to a trot. But instead of legs pairing in diagonals as in the trot, fore and hind legs on one side move together, giving a swaying action.

Slow gait – Four beats, but with swaying from side to side and a prancing effect. The slow gait is one of the gaits used by five-gaited saddle horses. Some call this pace the *stepping pace* or *amble*.

Amble – A slow, easy gait, much like the pace.

Rack – One of the five gaits of the five-gaited American saddle horse, it's a fancy, fast walk. This four-beat gait is faster than the trot and is very hard on the horse.

Jog – A jog is a slow trot, sometimes called a *dogtrot*.

Lope – A slow, easygoing canter, usually referring to a western gait on a horse ridden with loose reins.

Fox trot – An easy gait of short steps in which the horse basically walks in front and trots behind. It's a smooth gait, great for long-distance riding and characteristic of the Missouri fox trotter.

Parts of a Horse

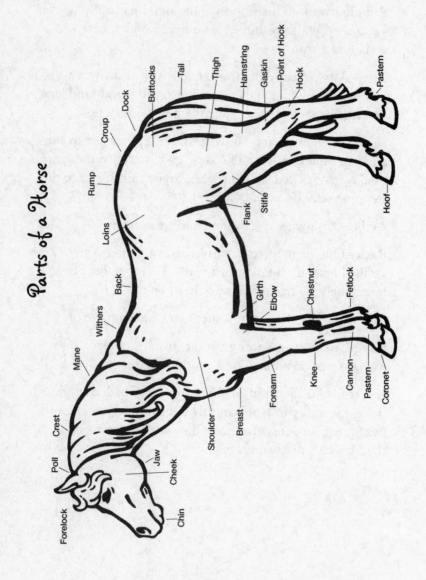

The Western Saddle

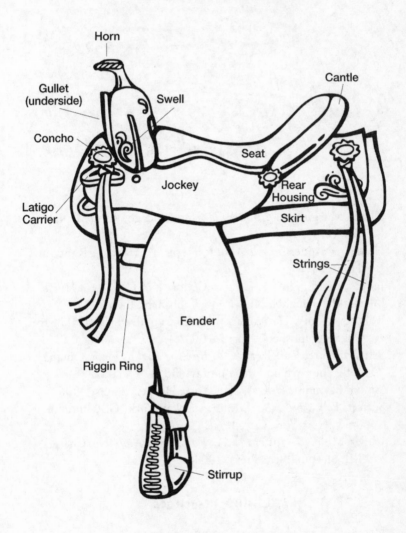

Horn

Gullet (underside)

Swell

Cantle

Concho

Seat

Jockey

Rear Housing

Latigo Carrier

Skirt

Strings

Fender

Riggin Ring

Stirrup

Resources for Horse Information Contained in this Book

Henry, Marguerite. *Album of Horses*. Chicago: Rand McNally & Co., 1952.

Henry, Marguerite. *All About Horses*. New York: Random House, 1967.

Jeffery, Laura. *Horses: How to Choose and Care for a Horse*. Berkley Heights, NJ: Enslow Publishers, Inc., 2004.

Roberts, Monty. *The Horses in My Life*. Pomfret, VT: Trafalgar Square Publishers, North, 2004.

Self, Margaret Cabell. *How to Buy the Right Horse*. Omaha, NE: The Farnam Horse Library, 1971.

Simon, Seymour. *Horses*. New York: HarperCollins, 2006.

Sutton, Felix. *Horses of America*. New York: G.P. Putnam's Sons, New York City, 1964.

Ulmer, Mike. *H is for Horse: An Equestrian Alphabet*. Chelsea, MI: Sleeping Bear Press, 2004.

Online resources

http://www.appaloosayouth.com/index.html
http://www.shetlandminiature.com/kids.asp
http://www.twhbea.com/youth/youthHome.aspx

Book 1: A Horse to Love

By Marsha Hubler

Softcover • ISBN 978-0-310-71792-8

Meet Skye, a troubled foster girl, sent to live with Christian foster parents who introduce her to the wonderful world of horses. At Keystone Stables, a special-needs dude
ranch in central Pennsylvania, Skye meets Champ, a champion sorrel quarter horse
who helps her accept God's unconditional forgiveness and love. Previously titled as
The Trouble with Skye.

Available now at your local bookstore!

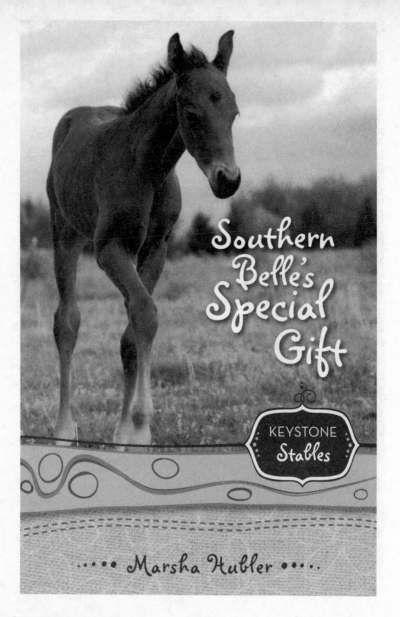

Book 3: Southern Belle's Special Gift

By Marsha Hubler

Softcover • ISBN 978-0-310-71794-2

Skye and Morgan have their hands full when a runaway named Tanya Bell becomes a foster girl in the Chambers' household. It isn't until Southern Belle, one of the mares, dies giving birth to a foal that Tanya opens up to the love offered from the Chambers' family. Previously titled as *Trouble Times Two*.

Coming October 2009

Book 4: Summer Camp Adventure

By Marsha Hubler

Softcover • ISBN 978-0-310-71795-9

For the summer, Skye and her school friend Chad work at Camp Lackawanna Falls special-needs camp. Skye runs into a brick wall when she tries to teach Jonathan Martin, a young deaf boy, how to ride his horse Buddy western style, while Jonathan insists on riding him English. When Jonathan and Buddy disappear into the mountains, Skye and Chad lead the rescue to find him. Previously titled as *Teamwork at Camp Tioga*.

Coming October 2009

Book 5: Leading the Way

By Marsha Hubler

Softcover • ISBN 978-0-310-71796-6

Skye is especially excited to help Katie Thomas, a girl who went blind in a car accident four years ago. As Skye shares God's love, Katie's faith begins to grow, and she gets swept up in the world of horses. After bonding with one horse, a brown-and-white Pinto named Boomerang, Katie soon learns to barrel race and, with Skye's help, deals with the threat of her parents' divorce. Previously titled as *The Winning Summer*.

Coming February 2010

Book 6: Blue Ribbon Champ

By Marsha Hubler

Softcover • ISBN 978-0-310-71797-3

Joey Klingerman, a visitor at Keystone Stables, has Down syndrome and is very outgoing and talkative. He immediately takes a special liking to Skye, constantly calling her his girlfriend. Embarrassed and furious, Skye begins to treat Joey harshly, but when Bucky, his buckskin horse, comes up lame right before the county fair, Skye is forced to make a big decision. Skye has to listen to God's promptings in order to share his love with Joey. Previously titled as *Skye's Final Test*.

Coming February 2010

ZONDERkidz
.com

Book 7: Whispering Hope

By Marsha Hubler
Softcover • ISBN 978-0-310-71691-4

Dad Chambers bought a wild pinto mustang, Rebel, at the auction, and the horse
seems to live up to his name. When Skye and Chad attempt to train Rebel, their horse-
whispering techniques fail, and Skye feels like giving up.

Coming May 2010

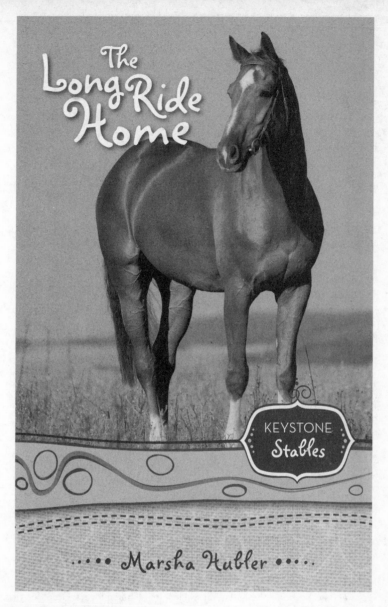

Book 8: The Long Ride Home
By Marsha Hubler
Softcover • ISBN 978-0-310-71692-1

Skye is happy living at Keystone Stables with her foster parents, Mr. and Mrs. Chambers, but she often wonders what her mom and dad are like. Some of her questions are answered when, while on a trip to a horse competition in South Carolina with the Chambers and Morgan, Skye meets an aunt she never knew she had. Millie Nicholson Eister helps Skye begin her search for her parents, whom Skye has not seen since she was a toddler.

Coming May 2010

Wild About Horses Bible
Softcover • ISBN 978-0-310-71730-0

What girl doesn't love horses? This NIV compact Bible includes beautiful color photographs and inspirational thoughts that will inspire all horse lovers. Great for girls on the go—on the road, in the back pack, or tucked under a saddle!

Features include:

- 12 beautiful full-color photos of horses
- Short inspirational thoughts and scripture verses on themes of love, peace, friendship, beauty, strength, and faith accompany the photos.
- Presentation page for gift giving
- The most-read, most-trusted New International Version
- Duo-tone leather binding with horse motif embossing

Available now at your local bookstore!